'I'm your husband!'

'You were never that.'

'We were married for two years—'

'*I* was married for two years,' she corrected him vehemently. 'You were still Adam Carmichael, stud extraordinaire!'

His hand gripped her wrist. 'Don't start believing all the drivel you've read about me—'

'I didn't need to read about it, Adam, I lived it!'

Carole Mortimer says: 'I was born in England, the youngest of three children—I have two older brothers. I started writing in 1978, and have now written over 90 books for Harlequin Mills & Boon.

'I have four sons—Matthew, Joshua, Timothy and Peter—and a bearded collie dog called Merlyn. I'm in a very happy relationship with Peter senior; we're best friends as well as lovers, which is probably the best recipe for a successful relationship. We live on the Isle of Man.'

Recent titles by the same author:

ONE-MAN WOMAN
WILDEST DREAMS

A MARRIAGE
TO REMEMBER

BY
CAROLE MORTIMER

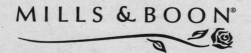

MILLS & BOON®

For Peter

First published in Great Britain 1997
Harlequin Mills & Boon Limited,
Eton House, 18-24 Paradise Road, Richmond, Surrey TW9 1SR

© Carole Mortimer 1997

ISBN 0 263 80456 9

Set in Times Roman 11 on 12 pt.
01-9711-47219 C1

Printed and bound in Great Britain
by Mackays of Chatham PLC, Chatham

CHAPTER ONE

HE STOOD at the back of the dimly lit, smoke-filled room, unnoticed by the crowd, especially the noisy people clamouring for attention at the bar beside him. But that was all right—they were completely unnoticed by him too.

Because he knew that as soon as the woman standing on the slightly raised dais across at the other side of the room began to sing again the crowd would forget their need for a drink, would fall into a hushed silence once more as they forgot everything but listening to the music.

She had been on stage for almost half an hour now, and it was the same each time she began to sing a new song; a pin could have been heard dropping amongst the appreciative audience. It was easy to understand why. She was good. Very good. As good as she ever had been, the haunting sensuality of her voice reaching out and touching a chord in the heart of each person in the room. She sang of love. Betrayed love. And yet there was also hope in her words. Hope of survival. And there was a joy in life itself. In the mere gift of life.

Where had she found such joy?

How?

Who with?

It was this last agonising question that ripped into him like the sharpness of a knife, that held him mesmerised as he stood silently watching the haunting beauty of her face.

Then the room fell silent around him once more as she began to lightly strum her guitar; it was an expectant silence, as if everyone in the room had suddenly held their breath at the same time.

He knew why. He too recognised those opening chords. And the words as she began to sing. It was a song he hadn't heard for a long time. A long, long time.

Their song...

CHAPTER TWO

HE WAS in the room. She couldn't see him. Had no idea where he was. She only knew she could feel him here. Somewhere.

She had felt his presence almost from the moment she had walked out in front of the audience, at first berating herself for her imaginings; it was ridiculous, after all this time, to feel that way. There was no logical reason to believe such a thing. But the feeling had persisted, to such an extent that she was now convinced he was definitely in the room. Listening to her.

It was incredible that she should feel like this. It was the first time she had sung in public for over three years; why would he be here?

But he was. She knew he was, had become more and more convinced of it as she continued to sing. She had looked searchingly through the crowd to see if she could recognise him, but it was difficult to see into the gloom beyond her spotlight. There were just silhouettes of people, with no distinguishing features at all.

She didn't want to recognise him anyway. What was the point? It was all so long ago now. She was different. He was different. Their lives were different.

But he was here...!

Her heart pounded in her chest—loudly, it seemed to her, as she began to play her final song for the evening, strumming the introduction on her guitar before she began to pick out the more recognisable chorus.

She wished the song weren't in the programme now, wished she had chosen to end with any other song but this one. But it was the song she was known for, the song people remembered her for. And she hadn't sung it in public for a long, long time.

Their song…

CHAPTER THREE

'YOU were brilliant, Maggi! Absolutely brilliant,' Mark enthused, his eyes shining. 'I—'

'Adam is here.' She flatly cut across his enthusiastic exuberance, automatically handing him her guitar for him to put it away in the waiting case.

Mark froze in the action, frowning darkly. 'Adam...?' he repeated disbelievingly.

'Can we just get out of here?' she said agitatedly, pushing back the swathe of long straight hair that had fallen over the slenderness of one shoulder—hair as black as a raven's wing.

'But—'

'Now, Mark!' Maggi insisted firmly, snapping shut her guitar case before picking it up in preparation for leaving the room she had retreated to after leaving the stage seconds ago.

He still didn't move, smiling at her sympathetically, well aware of the strain she had been under tonight. 'I understand how you feel, Maggi.' He squeezed her arm. 'But Adam can't be here—'

'I'm telling you he is!' she bit out between gritted teeth, deep blue eyes flashing a warning of just how close to breaking point she was. In fact, if they didn't get out of this club soon, she was going to scream! Adam was here somewhere—she just knew he was— and he was the last person she wanted to see tonight, of all nights. 'I know how unlikely it is,' she acknowledged heavily. 'How ridiculous it sounds. But, believe me, he is here!'

She'd had trouble believing it herself as she was singing, had thought it was perhaps just her imagination; after all, in the past Adam had always been with her when she sang. In fact, it had seemed strange to her, at the start of this evening, that he wasn't there. But she had been wrong about that; he had been here, and she had become more and more convinced of that as the minutes passed. She had barely been able to suppress her panic in order to finish her spot on stage, and she desperately wanted to get away now, didn't want to actually be put in a position where she would have to see him. Knowing he was here was enough…!

Mark frowned again. 'But listen to that audience, Maggi.' The applause could still be heard from the adjoining club-room. 'They want you back on stage.'

The audience, a welcoming audience earlier this evening, were going wild, calling her name, demanding she come back and sing them another song. But she couldn't do it. Not now she was convinced Adam was out there too.

She shook her head, her small, heart-shaped face as pale as alabaster against the framing blackness of her hair. 'Maybe tomorrow night, Mark,' she dismissed huskily. 'I've had enough for one evening.'

It had been a strain for her, going back in front of an audience after all this time, which was why this particular venue, as opposed to a big concert hall, had been chosen in the first place: a music festival in a small town in the north of England, where her name could be lost amongst those of other artists appearing in the three-day event. The venues were informal—

clubs, pubs, meeting-rooms—with several concerts taking place at the same time. It was exactly the right sort of place for Maggi to make her first public reappearance.

Or at least it would have been—if she hadn't been utterly convinced that Adam was out there in the audience. Watching her. The very last person she wanted near her during her first public appearance for three years!

Mark looked at her closely, finally nodding his agreement to their leaving as he recognised the signs of strain around her eyes and mouth. 'You've done well for your first night, Maggi,' he told her with bright encouragement as they turned to leave. 'But you'll do even better tomorrow night—because by then it will be all around the festival that you're back and greater than ever!' he said confidently.

She wasn't too sure about the latter, although she had to concede that the audience had been an appreciative one. She had been very nervous when she'd begun her spot for the evening, but from the onset had felt the audience's warmth reaching out to her, welcoming her, and that nervousness had almost completely disappeared as they'd clapped and cheered after each song. Yes, this festival had been a good choice as a place for her to resume her career.

If only she didn't have that nagging, uneasy feeling inside her that told her Adam was near...

Mark covered her own numbed silence on the journey back to their hotel by talking all the time, obviously pleased with the way the evening had gone. He had good reason to be; without his help and constant encouragement this evening would probably never have happened. Mark had been her emotional support over the last few years, always there when she needed a boost to her flagging morale; for his sake alone she was pleased that this appearance seemed to have gone so well.

They had chosen to stay in a big impersonal hotel just outside of town rather than in one of the busier places actually in the centre, where, for all that she had disappeared from the music scene for the last three years, it was likely she would be recognised by people attending the festival. She was nervous enough already, without having to put on a front for people who might want to talk to her.

'The key to your suite, Miss Fennell?' The receptionist gave her a bright, welcoming smile before turning to take the key from the hook behind her. 'Oh, and something arrived for you earlier, but I'm afraid you had already left the hotel when it was delivered...'

Maggi paled as the other woman turned back to hand her a long, cellophane-wrapped box decorated with a red ribbon, already able to guess, from its appearance alone, exactly what it contained. A single red rose...

'Thank you.' Mark was the one to almost snatch the box out of the receptionist's hands, clasping Maggi's elbow with his other hand as he walked her over to the lift, looking down at her in concern as he did so.

Her eyes were huge in the paleness of her face, deeply blue and haunted. She was expressionless, too shocked to feel anything at this precise moment in time. It hadn't been her imagination at all that Adam was here. He really was. The rose proved that.

Always, in the past, on the night of a performance, Adam would arrange for a single red rose to be delivered to her dressing-room at the start of the evening. As he had arranged for one to be brought to her hotel this evening...

He knew where she was staying!

Her expression was panicked as she turned to the man at her side. 'Mark—'

'It's all right, Maggi,' he soothed as he let them both into the suite. 'It's only a rose.' Even as he spoke he smoothly dropped the red-ribbon-wrapped box into the bin just inside the sitting-room. 'As easily disposed of as that,' he added with satisfaction.

Maggi conceded that the flower might be easily disposed of, but she knew the man who'd sent it wasn't. At least, the memory of him wasn't. She had spent the last three years attempting to bury every memory of him—and the single act of sending her a red rose had brought all those memories flooding back. And the pain that went along with them.

Mark watched her as she slowly sat down in one of the armchairs. He was a tall, dark-haired man, a couple of years older than Maggi's own twenty-six.

'Maggi, don't let him ruin this for you.' Mark came down on his haunches beside her chair to take her hands into his much larger ones. Her fingers were chilled against his, despite the relative warmth of the autumn evening. 'God knows, he's already taken enough from you!' he added with grim fierceness.

She swallowed hard, trying to rid herself of feelings of nausea. While there had still been some doubt, while she had been able to half convince herself she was imagining Adam's presence tonight, to tell herself she had just *thought* he was there because he always had been in the past, she had been able to keep her emotions under control. But now there was no doubt…!

She looked at Mark with haunted eyes. 'Why is he here, Mark?' Her voice was huskily soft, filled with pain.

His hands tightened about hers. 'Why was he ever anywhere?' he returned bitterly, shaking his head. 'If not to cause trouble?'

'But why?' she groaned brokenly. 'What did I ever do to him that he should want to hurt me again now?'

She hadn't seen or heard from Adam in three years, and yet the first time she made a public appearance… How could he do this to her, after all he had already done in the past?

'That's it, Maggi,' Mark encouraged as he saw the flash of anger that suddenly lightened her eyes. 'Don't get sad, get mad! That bastard has caused you enough damage without trying to ruin this for you too!'

Mark was right, and despite her nervousness earlier this evening, about appearing in public again, she had also been looking forward to it in a way, to seeing if she could really still do it. And she had. She could!

That red rose might have shaken her, but Mark was also right when he said she couldn't let that take any of her earlier triumph away from her. She had another two days of the festival to get through, when, she admitted, there was a possibility of bumping into Adam. But she was at least aware of his presence now, was prepared for it, even if she accepted that facing him again would probably be the hardest thing she would ever have to do in her life.

But she could do it. She had survived, had got through the initial difficulty of this evening too; she could certainly get through seeing Adam again.

She squared her shoulders determinedly, giving Mark a bright smile. 'Let's order a bottle of champagne to celebrate this evening!' She stood up, determined to shake off the despondency that had fallen upon them both since they had seen the rose.

Mark stood up too, grinning, obviously relieved she had decided to rise to the occasion. 'I thought you would never ask!'

They were both acting a role. Maggi accepted that, knew that with the worry of Adam's presence somewhere in the area neither of them particularly felt like celebrating anything. But it was a role both of them were going to play, and, without another glance at the box containing the rose, Maggi telephoned Room Service to order the champagne.

Thoughts of Adam could come later, when she couldn't put them off any longer. For the moment she only wanted to think of the success of the evening just gone. And to share that success with Mark.

'The place is packed, Maggi!' Mark told her excitedly the following evening as she stood waiting to go out on stage.

She could hear the sound of the audience talking loudly together as they waited for her to make an appearance, knew by the volume of noise that the large civic hall, where she was to perform tonight, must indeed be very full.

'I told you this was what would happen once people heard of your success last night,' Mark continued happily. 'You're on your way back, Maggi!' He gave her a hug.

Her way back to where? That was what she was starting to worry about. She had been working hard towards this weekend—a long, uphill struggle that she had finally won. But if it meant she might have to see Adam again...

That was something that had never even entered her head, not at the beginning, or during those past months of planning. She'd had no reason to suppose he would want to see her again, any more than she wanted to see him. But last night he had sent that red rose...

And tonight, before she and Mark had left the hotel, there had been another rose, letting her know more forcefully than anything else could have done that Adam knew she was singing again this evening.

'Try to look more cheerful about it,' Mark reproved her now frowningly. 'This is what you've worked so hard for.'

He was right; she knew he was. She couldn't let Adam spoil this for her. As he had spoilt so many things before...

She had been in trepidation earlier today that Adam might turn up at the hotel looking for her. But the time had passed in relative peace, their food delivered by Room Service, she and Mark only leaving the suite for a couple of hours this afternoon to go and luxuriate in the hotel pool—and she had started to relax.

But would Adam be out there again tonight? It was logical to assume he probably would be; it was listed in the festival's weekend programme exactly when and where she would be playing over the three-day period. It was the thought of him standing silently in the audience watching her, when she couldn't see him—as she still felt sure he had been last night!—that was so unnerving to her. The second single rose that had been delivered to the hotel earlier seemed to be a promise of that, despite Mark's protestations that she should just forget about it, forget about Adam. He knew better than most how she had tried to do that—he must also know how impossible she had found it to do!

Mark grasped her firmly by the tops of her arms, forcing her to look up into his boyishly handsome face. 'Remember, Maggi, don't get sad, get mad,' he reminded her. 'Don't give Adam the satisfaction of ruining anything else for you.'

It came as no surprise to her that Mark knew exactly what—who!—was bothering her; they had always been close, but even more so recently, with Mark often seeming to know what she was thinking before she was aware of it herself.

'You're right.' She straightened determinedly, a diminutive figure dressed completely in black: flat ankle boots, denims, a silk shirt open at the throat, and her long, almost waist-length hair cascading down her spine. Long silver earrings dangled against her neck, the only jewellery she wore; her slender wrists and hands were completely bare of adornment. She reached up to kiss Mark lightly on the cheek. 'Time to go on!' She gave him a brightly reassuring smile.

The hall was much bigger than the club last night, but as Maggi stepped out onto the stage she could see it was packed with people—people who began to clap and cheer as soon as they saw her. Her nervousness instantly fell away at this spontaneous reception, professionalism taking over, and she smiled confidently at the crowd as she began to play the opening chords to her first song.

She tried not to search the sea of faces as she performed, dreading and yet looking for that all too familiar face. But there were so many people here tonight, so many positive responses coming her way as she sang song after song, that in the end she had to give up looking. It would serve no useful purpose even if she could locate Adam in the crowd. In fact, it would have the opposite effect!

She was on for longer tonight, over an hour in all, and it felt like old times as she enjoyed herself as much as the audience obviously did.

And then the catastrophe happened!

It wasn't such an unusual thing. Wasn't really such a catastrophe. It was just the last thing she would have wanted to happen this evening. A string broke on the guitar she was playing—her favourite guitar. Her spare guitar was out in the room she had waited in earlier before coming on stage.

She glanced across at Mark where he stood in the wings watching her, acknowledging his nod of understanding before he strode off to get her other guitar, and turned to put her useless instrument back on the stand behind her. She would just have to sing the next song unaccompanied.

There was a ripple of sympathy amongst the audience as they recognised her dilemma, and they gave her an encouraging round of applause before she began to sing. Her voice was clear, the trueness of the notes reaching every corner of the room, and the silence was appreciative as the hush washed over the hall.

Then Maggi realised she was no longer singing unaccompanied, and that she recognised the guitar work she could hear only too well.

She turned sharply to her left, only to have her worst suspicions confirmed as to exactly why the audience had suddenly fallen so silent; Adam had walked onto the stage behind her, and it was his guitar she could now hear accompanying her.

Maggi hadn't seen him in such a long time, and as she looked at him now she could see the changes in him. His dark hair was longer than it had been, with flecks of grey amongst its thickness. His eyes were still as dark a grey, but there were lines beneath them; and grooved into his cheeks beside his mouth, a mouth set grimly, as was the arrogant angle of his jaw.

He was dressed almost exactly the same as Maggi, in black denims and a black silk shirt, the latter unbuttoned from his throat to reveal the growth of dark hair on his chest. This was the way he had always dressed when they'd sung together in the past.

He looked at Maggi challengingly as her singing faltered at the sight of him beside her, and she knew exactly why he was frowning at her so darkly; 'the show must go on' had always been Adam's attitude. No matter what the circumstances. As Maggi knew to her cost...

Adam continued to play the melody on his guitar, still looking at her expectantly, his dark gaze compelling her to begin singing again, to give the audience what they had come here for.

But he was wrong. The audience weren't waiting for the song to resume. Their stunned silence at Adam's unexpected appearance was replaced by whispered conversations now as they all wanted to confirm that it really was Adam Carmichael standing up on the stage beside Maggi Fennell.

Maggi was having trouble believing it herself! She had known he was here in the hall—the second rose had told her that only too clearly—but she had never guessed he would actually have the nerve to join her on the stage.

How dared he? As Mark had said, 'Don't get sad, get mad.' And she was *mad*—in fact she was furious. How dared Adam do this to her?

'Sing, damn it!' he muttered between gritted teeth, while keeping up a completely impersonal expression for the people who were looking at the two of them so curiously now.

Sing! She wasn't sure a sound would pass her lips, let alone any that would actually be in tune. They hadn't stood together on a stage like this for so long, she—

'I said sing!' he grated again, playing the introduction to the song once again.

Maggi could see Mark at the side of the stage, holding her second guitar in his hand, knew he was riveted to the spot as he saw who was standing beside her. But he had to know, too, that there was nothing he could do about Adam's presence either, not without causing a scene. And that was the last thing any of them wanted in front of so many people.

But she needed her guitar if she was to continue—

if only as something for her to hold onto! She quickly crossed the stage to take the instrument from Mark's unresisting fingers.

'What the hell—?' Mark muttered furiously as he looked across at the other man.

Maggi shook her head wordlessly. For the moment there was nothing either of them could do about this situation; she just had to get on with the performance. What happened after that was anybody's guess!

Her smile was one of complete professionalism as she turned back to face the audience, her gaze having passed sightlessly over Adam; if she didn't look at him, maybe she would be able to get through this. Maybe...

She began to sing, accompanying herself on the guitar, aware that her own guitar work was not as good as Adam's more intricate style. But then, it never had been; their styles had always complemented each other, had never been the same.

Adam had chosen to play—deliberately, so it seemed to Maggi—one of the songs they'd used to sing together, and as they approached the chorus she waited tensely for Adam to join in the harmony. His voice had always been rich and deep, a perfect contrast for her higher, throaty voice.

Even Maggi felt the goose-bumps down her spine as the two of them harmonised perfectly. God, it was as if they had never stopped singing together, as if they had been practising this song for weeks in the build-up to the music festival. And instead they hadn't even seen each other for three years, hadn't sung together for a long time before that...

The audience went wild with appreciation as the

last notes trailed off the guitars, instantly recognising the perfection of Maggi and Adam's performance. But it had always been like this between them on stage, a complete rapport, an understanding that went so much deeper than the music.

But Maggi still couldn't bring herself to look at Adam, her heart sinking as the audience shouted for more. Not that she blamed any of these people for their enthusiasm; they were witnessing an event that had never been expected to happen again—Adam Carmichael and Maggi Fennell singing together once more.

'"Home Town",' Adam prompted softly at her side, mentioning a song the two of them had recorded together several years ago, a song that had once been very successful for them.

She looked at him sharply, making no effort to comply with the command. 'I don't need you any more, Adam,' she returned as softly. Both were aware of the live microphones in front of them.

His expression hardened; his grey eyes narrowed. 'You never did. But at the moment we have an audience to please,' he muttered harshly. '"Home Town",' he repeated, with a firmness that brooked no argument, instantly launching into the fast introduction to the song.

All of this was beyond Maggi's worst nightmares, and how she managed to get through the next thirty minutes she had no idea. But the audience were wild with joy, refusing to let them stop, demanding song after song, most of which Maggi had thought she would never, ever sing again.

She did all of it without looking at Adam—found

she couldn't look at him; it brought back too many memories. Memories she would rather forget...

'We've gone over our time,' she finally told him flatly as she pulled the guitar strap over her head, a signal to the audience, too, that she had finished. She flicked back the shining length of her hair.

Adam kept his guitar strap over his shoulder. 'They want more,' he pointed out dryly. Most of the audience were on their feet now, sensing they were going to lose the highlight of the evening, probably of the whole festival, and unwilling to relinquish such a treat.

Maggi's blue eyes flashed as she looked across at him. 'There are other people waiting to perform,' she reminded him stiffly. The next performer had been standing in the wings for the last ten minutes, and was talking animatedly to Mark now—a Mark who didn't look too responsive to whatever was being said to him as his gaze remained fixed fiercely on Maggi and Adam.

Adam glanced across at the two men in the wings too, ignoring Mark's scowling face and grinning his satisfaction when the other man gestured his willingness for Maggi and Adam to continue. 'He doesn't seem to mind,' Adam told Maggi with satisfaction.

'But—'

'"Passing Years", Magdalena,' Adam insisted challengingly.

Only Adam had ever called her by the name chosen by her Spanish mother; most people, her English father and even her mother, preferred to call her by the shortened version of Maggi. His use of her full name was enough to evoke even stronger memories of Adam and herself.

As was his suggestion that they sing 'their song'...

She could feel her face pale even at the thought. She had sung it last night because it had been expected of her. But then she had sung it alone. She never wanted to perform that particular song with Adam again. It was too— She just couldn't sing it with him!

'You can, Magdalena,' Adam bit out harshly, and Maggi realised she must have unwittingly spoken her protest out loud. 'You can do anything you damn well want to!' he added grimly.

She looked at him sharply, at the accusation in his cold grey eyes. 'I don't want to do this,' she told him furiously.

'Stop acting like a spoilt child, Magdalena.' The coldness of his tone was like a slap in the face. 'You chose to come back, to put yourself in the public eye again, and now you have to give them what they want!'

It was obvious, from the shouted encouragement of the audience, that what they wanted was for Adam and Maggi to continue—all night if possible. It was also obvious that Adam was quite happy to do that.

It had always been like this with Adam; everyone else's feelings had always meant more to him than hers. He hadn't changed, would never change.

'All right, Adam, we'll do this one last song,' she finally conceded flatly, swinging her guitar strap back over her head onto her slender shoulder. 'And then I'm leaving the stage. After that I don't ever want to see you again.' Her voice was strong and unyielding, but the words sounded childish in their intensity. But it was the truth; once she left this stage this evening she didn't want Adam anywhere near her.

'The first you may be able to do,' he murmured softly, before turning back to the waiting audience. 'The second you may not have any choice about,' he added grimly.

Maggi looked at him sharply; exactly what did he mean by that last remark?

CHAPTER FOUR

'I CAN'T believe he did that!' Mark strode angrily up
and down in their hotel suite. 'I just couldn't believe
it was actually him up on the stage with you when I
came back from the dressing-room with your guitar.
Arrogant bastard!' He shook his head, as if he still
couldn't quite take in what he had seen.

Maggi could easily understand his anger and dis-
belief; she was sure a lot of other people who had
been in that hall tonight were still stunned at having
seen Adam Carmichael.

As she was!

It all seemed like a dream now that they were back
at their hotel, Maggi having escaped from the stage
at the end of 'their song', glancing back only once,
to see that Adam wasn't having the same success in
leaving, the audience calling for more, refusing to let
him go. And with good reason; Adam was, and always had been, a phenomenon in his own right. He
had gone on in the last three years to be an entertainer
much in demand all over the world. The audience tonight had been more than aware of just how privileged
they were to hear him sing so unexpectedly.

But Maggi could well have done without it, and
was still shaken by the way he had joined her on stage
in that autocratic way. But then, he always had been
the most arrogant man she'd ever met in her life; he
didn't believe any of the rules were meant for him,

26

living his life by his own set of codes—and they were like no one else's. When Maggi had first met him she had believed his arrogance to be self-confidence, had felt protected by it—it had only been later that she had learnt, to her cost, just how wrong she was...!

'He ruined your comeback, damn him!' Mark continued furiously. 'You were going to do this on your own, and now he's—'

'What's done is done, Mark.' She sat in one of the armchairs, exhausted, mainly by all the emotional trauma of the evening. 'There's nothing we can do to change that,' she added wearily, knowing beyond a shadow of a doubt that the music festival had turned into a fiasco as far as the return of her music career went.

It had all been planned so carefully, the whole thing to be taken slowly: the music festival this weekend, a couple of other low-key gigs lined up for next month—nothing too exacting, just a slow introduction back into the world she loved best. But if the Press got to hear of the performance with Adam this evening...!

'I can't do the third evening tomorrow, Mark,' she told him.

Mark stopped his pacing and looked across at her. 'You have to, Maggi.' He frowned. 'You're billed to appear and people will be expecting to hear you.' Mark was another person who believed that the public must be given what they wanted.

She shook her head, a rueful smile on her lips. 'They will be expecting to hear Adam too now,' she pointed out with a heavy sigh. 'And they will be disappointed,' she added determinedly; there was no way

she was going to perform tomorrow evening and have
Adam do to her again what he had done tonight. 'I—'
She broke off as a knock sounded firmly on the door
of their hotel suite, her eyes wide as she gave a startled look in its direction.

She didn't need two guesses as to who was standing
on the other side of it; Adam had obviously managed
to find her at last. She didn't want to see him just
now. If ever!

'It's Adam,' she told Mark with certainty, standing
up abruptly. 'I don't want to see him, Mark.' She gave
a shake of her head.

Mark's mouth was set angrily, blue eyes blazing as
he too turned towards the door. 'But I do!' he grated.
'I—'

'Then you see him,' she dismissed agitatedly as that
knock sounded firmly again. 'I'm going to my room.'
She turned quickly on her heel.

'This had to happen some time, Maggi,' Mark
called after her softly. 'Isn't it better to get it over
with now?'

Speak to Adam? Be close to him once again? Know
the full force of his personality? Know she had once
loved him to distraction? Until he had destroyed that
love as callously as he might have swatted a fly, when
it no longer suited him to have her love. To look at
him again and know all that?

'No!' she told Mark with a shudder of revulsion.
'It isn't better to ''get it over with now''. I was over
Adam a long time ago, said everything that needed to
be said then; I have no reason to ever see him again!'
She strode determinedly from the room, unwilling to
listen to any more arguments for reason from Mark,

closed her bedroom door behind her and sat down heavily on the bed, because her legs were shaking too much to support her, reaction having set in with a vengeance.

She had sung on a stage with Adam this evening— something she had been sure would never happen again. Something she had sworn would never happen again!

Even now she still had trouble believing it *had* happened. It had been just like old times, their voices harmonising as if it were only yesterday when they'd last sung together.

They had been the perfect couple, both on and off the stage. Everyone had said so. The love they had shared had deepened their performance when they'd sung together. Until tragedy had struck so unexpectedly and Maggi could no longer sing at Adam's side. It had been then, when she'd already felt as if she was in the depths of despair, that she had learnt all too forcibly just how tenuous the love that Adam had professed to feel for her was.

She could hear the murmur of voices in the other room, knew that whatever Mark had said when he opened the door to Adam it hadn't been enough to get the other man to leave. Not that she would have expected it to be. Adam had been arrogant enough three years ago; his solo success since that time had probably just made him more so!

Mark's voice was rising in anger now, and Maggi felt herself cringe inside as she heard the slow coldness with which Adam made his replies. He always had been able to rip a person to shreds with that icy control, and no matter how angry Mark might be, and however justified his anger, Maggi knew he was no match for Adam's cool determination.

Mark's voice seemed to be getting louder. 'I've told you, Adam—'

'I don't give a damn what you've told me,' Adam returned harshly. 'I intend to see Magdalena before I leave.' Even as he made this last statement the bedroom door was flung open, Adam almost filling the doorway as he stood there, his six-foot-four height only inches away from the top of the doorframe.

'Nice bedroom,' he drawled mockingly as he strolled nonchalantly into the room, just as if it hadn't been ages since they had last spoken, as if there hadn't been all that heartache with the passing of those years. 'I'm sure the two of you are very comfortable here,' he added hardly, grey eyes still icy cold as he met Maggi's rebellious gaze. 'You always did like your creature comforts, didn't you, Magdalena? And a nice big bed was one of them.' He looked pointedly at the king-size bed she still sat on. 'Preferably with a man inside it!' he added harshly.

Maggi gasped at his insulting tone, and in the outer room she could see Mark's hands clench into fists at his sides; she knew that his volatile temper was in danger of exploding. But it would be no match for the freezing concentration of Adam's!

She drew in a deep breath and stood up, feeling at a complete disadvantage sitting on the bed. Not that standing up made too much difference to that; Adam always had had the ability to make her look—and feel!—like a little girl disguised as a woman, her shortness and slenderness of frame emphasised by his height and sheer masculinity.

'How right you are,' she returned, sounding much more calm than she actually felt. 'But I do draw the line at having two men in my bedroom at the same time!' she told him levelly, walking over to the doorway where Mark still stood. 'Shall we all go through to the lounge?' She looked at them both pointedly.

Adam shrugged broad shoulders beneath his black silk shirt. 'I'm quite happy for this conversation to take place in there,' he dismissed with a mocking twist of his lips. 'It was your boyfriend here who had a problem with it.' He looked contemptuously down his aristocratic nose at Mark as he strode past him; he was several inches taller than the younger man, despite Mark's own six feet in height.

Maggi walked slowly back into the sitting-room, aware of the two men behind her; they were so different as to be almost opposites. Mark was easygoing, comfortable to be with, undemanding, whereas Adam, ten years his senior, had never been any of those things; he was the most demanding man she had ever met, and, far from finding him comfortable to be with, she had always been very aware of him in every way, her senses constantly alive to his mere presence.

Which was probably why she had been so sure last night that he was at this music festival; she had sensed he was there!

'You're looking well, Magdalena,' Adam told her softly once they were all assembled in the sitting-room.

That name again!

She sat down in one of the armchairs, more tired from the strain of the evening than she cared to admit. She sat forward in the chair, unable to relax, the darkness of her hair falling forward over her shoulders. 'How did you expect me to look, Adam?' she returned scornfully, deep blue eyes clashing with icy grey. 'Broken and defeated?' As she had undoubtedly been on the day he'd left her life three years ago!

At the time she hadn't believed, after what had already happened to her, that her life could get any worse than it already was; how wrong she had been! She hadn't allowed for Adam, for his cold selfishness.

His mouth tightened. 'No, I—'

'As you can see, Adam—' Mark was the one to interrupt him '—Maggi is happy and well—and doing just fine without you!' he added challengingly.

Glacial eyes were turned in his direction. 'When I want your opinion, dear cousin—' Adam drawled the last two words insultingly '—I'll ask for it! At this moment I happen to be talking to Magdalena.'

Cousin. Yes, these men were first cousins. It was hard to believe they could be related, that their mothers had been sisters, but it had been through her friendship with Mark that she had first met Adam, having accompanied the younger man to a family wedding. Adam had got up to sing during the reception and Mark had encouraged Maggi to join him. Even then, though their performance was completely unrehearsed, it had been obvious to the people listening that there was something magical about the two of them singing together.

Adam had been at the wedding with his long-term girlfriend, Jane, and Maggi had been dating Mark for almost six months. But something had happened between the two of them that day, and when Adam had telephoned her a couple of days later, having got her number from Mark, and suggested they go through some songs together with the intention of actually performing them in front of an audience in the future, Maggi had felt no hesitation in agreeing to meet him.

If only she had hesitated! If only she could have known the heartache that would follow, then she would never, ever have gone near Adam after that telephone call.

'As Mark has already told you,' she firmly answered Adam now, 'I am very well, thank you.'

Adam's mouth twisted again at the formality of her tone. 'I'm so glad!' he returned tauntingly.

Her head went back challengingly. 'Are you?'

Adam's jaw tensed, a warning of his building anger. 'What sort of question is that? Of course I'm glad you're fit and well again,' he bit out harshly.

'I would have thought Maggi's scepticism was only too well deserved,' Mark derided dismissively. 'You haven't exactly been falling over yourself with concern for her welfare in the last three years!'

Adam was very still, a nerve pulsing in his now tightly clenched jaw, the lines beside his nose and mouth, acquisitions of those years, becoming more pronounced. 'And just how would you know what I have been doing?' he grated accusingly. 'You seem to have had your hands full during that time bedding Magdalena!'

'Mark, no!' Maggi had time to shout before she rushed across the room to stop his fist actually making contact with Adam, managing to put a restraining hand on his arm. 'He isn't worth it, Mark,' she told him quietly, her gaze softly compelling on his flushed face. 'He never was,' she added heavily, knowing it was true.

It had taken her a long time to accept it—weeks, months of pain and disillusionment, before realising that after two years of living her life for and with Adam he was no longer there for her, not physically or emotionally. That perhaps he never had been.

It was said that you never knew the extent of a person's love until faced with adversity; Adam had turned and walked away the first time their relationship had come up against a serious obstacle.

She turned to look at him as he stood so mockingly in front of Mark. 'Our relationship is none of your concern, Adam,' she told him flatly. 'Nothing that has happened in my life over the last three years is,' she added determinedly.

Adam's mouth curved wryly. 'I've been waiting most of that time for some family announcement of a wedding between the two of you.' He looked at them both coldly. 'Or did she turn you down a second time, Mark?' he added scornfully.

Again Maggi put a restraining hand on Mark's arm. Adam had always liked to bait the younger man. The friendship she'd had with his cousin before knowing him had always been a sore point with him, even though it had been Adam she had loved. It was true that perhaps if she had never met Adam she might have one day married Mark. But she *had* met Adam, and so the question of any marriage between herself and Mark was now ridiculous. As Adam must know only too well. He was just playing his games again— and she, for one, did not want to play!

'Mark and I don't need marriage to cement our relationship.' Again Maggi was the one to answer him. 'We know how we feel about each other,' she added challengingly, feeling some of the tension leave Mark as her hand still rested on his arm.

Adam's mouth thinned disapprovingly. 'So does everyone else when the two of you are openly staying here together!' He looked around him pointedly.

'Moral indignation, Adam?' Mark taunted, completely in control again now, squeezing Maggi's hand in thanks for her support before moving slightly away. 'That's rich, coming from you.' He looked at the other man contemptuously.

Neither Maggi nor Mark, she was sure, had any intention of telling Adam that this suite had two bedrooms: one for Mark and one for herself. If he chose to believe the two of them shared the bedroom they had just left, then that was Adam's problem. He only had his own warped morals by which to judge other people...

Adam looked coldly at the younger man for several seconds before slowly turning back to Maggi. 'I didn't come here to talk to the monkey,' he bit out disgustedly, his gaze dark on Maggi's face now. 'I spoke to the organisers of the festival after you left earlier,' he told her smoothly. 'They were very pleased with the way things went this evening.'

'You had no right to talk to any—'

'I'm sure they were,' Maggi interrupted Mark's angry outburst, glaring steadily at Adam.

He nodded unconcernedly. 'They would like us to repeat the performance tomorrow evening.'

'No,' she told him flatly, having already guessed what he was going to say; the organisers of the festival would be very silly not to try and cash in on the fact that Adam Carmichael was willing to perform. 'For one thing, I'm sure a world-famous celebrity like yourself must have a more pressing engagement—'

'None that I can think of,' he dismissed easily, looking at her challengingly now, hands thrust deeply into the pockets of his black trousers.

'And for another,' she continued as if he hadn't interrupted, 'I'm a solo performer myself now. I don't sing with anyone else.' It was a flat statement of fact which held no challenge. 'The organisers either accept that, and I go on stage alone tomorrow evening, or I don't perform at all,' she added.

His mouth twisted. 'You're better than you ever were, Magdalena,' he acknowledged dryly. 'So I'm sure they will accept that.'

'Then there's no problem, is there?' She gave him a humourless smile, immune to his praise, knowing that it was being given on a purely professional level; that was one area where Adam was always completely objective. As she knew only too well.

He shrugged those broad shoulders. 'The problem is, we were always better together than apart.'

Maggi drew in a harsh breath. 'It's a little late in the day for you to realise that!' she snapped scornfully.

'I always knew it, Magdalena,' he told her softly. 'It's just that there were commitments three years ago, commitments you weren't able to meet—'

'You know damn well why she wasn't able to meet them!' Mark exploded. 'Good God, man, she—'

'That's all old ground, Mark,' she interrupted firmly, her voice a little shriller than she would have wished. But to talk of the past was still hurtful for her; she couldn't deal with it objectively. 'It certainly has no relevance to here and now. It must be all too obvious that we have completely separate lives now, Adam. And I want it to continue that way,' she added hardly. Knowing Adam in the past had ultimately brought her only pain; she had no illusions left where he was concerned. She certainly didn't want her life involved with his again—not in any way!

'Musically—'

'Musically too,' she cut in. 'It's late, Adam,' she continued. 'It's been a long day, and I would like to get some sleep.'

He made no move to leave. 'You do realise there are bound to be repercussions from our being on stage together tonight?'

She wasn't so naive that she didn't realise their joint performance this evening would give rise to speculation about a new merging of talents; she just didn't want to deal with it now. Certainly not when Adam was present!

'I think the only repercussion that is likely to occur as a result of tonight's one-off performance,' Mark cut in dismissively, 'is that the general public will see that Maggi Fennell and Adam Carmichael are—publicly, at least—friends again, despite all the media speculation.' His mouth twisted. 'Privately, of course, it's a completely different story!' He turned to comfort Maggi. 'I don't think too much harm will come out of this evening, love,' he assured her gently.

'You're a fool, Mark,' the older man told him coldly. 'But then, you always were. Magdalena—'

'Get out of here, Adam,' Mark bit out shortly.

'I—'

'Can't you see Maggi has had enough?' the younger man interjected forcefully.

She could feel Adam's gaze on her now, didn't need to look at him to know he was looking at her. And she knew what he would see, knew that her face was pale, ethereally so, her eyes made to look even darker because of the shadows beneath them. She had never been particularly robust before her illness, but now her health was delicate to say the least. Tonight had been a strain she could well have done without.

'You're right,' Adam finally, grudgingly conceded. 'I'll come back in the morning, for breakfast, and we can talk about this then—'

'No!' Mark was right; she had had enough. By rights Adam shouldn't even be here, let alone be dictating what they would and wouldn't do. Her eyes flashed. 'I've told you, Adam.' She looked at him unblinkingly. 'We have nothing left to say to each other. About anything,' she added to save his protests. 'I don't want you to come back here, tomorrow or any other time. Now, if you'll both excuse me, I'm tired and I'm going to bed.' She didn't wait for a response from either man, turning sharply on her heel and going back to her bedroom.

It was only as she closed the door thankfully behind her that she realised she must have stopped breathing during that short walk to the bedroom; she gasped air into her starved lungs as she leant back against the door.

Seeing Adam up on the stage had been one thing but having him here in her hotel suite was something else entirely, his proximity bringing back memories she had deliberately buried in the back of her mind. She'd had to. For her own sanity. To think of the better times, the happier times with Adam, when she'd been so ill and desperate for him, would have driven her completely insane!

She sat on the bed as she heard the murmur of male voices again outside, then the firm closing of the suite door seconds later. Adam had gone…!

'Come in,' she called as a soft knock on her bedroom door followed his exit from the suite. She smiled wanly at Mark as he came concernedly into the room. 'He's gone?'

'Yes,' Mark rasped.

She nodded. 'Let's not have an inquest about it, hmm, and just hope we've seen the last of him?' That would perhaps be too much to hope for; Adam no doubt had other ideas on the subject. But there was always the possibility that he would one day do something completely unselfish and surprise her!

'I don't understand what he's doing here; my mother said he was in America,' Mark muttered irritatedly.

Maggi raised startled brows. 'Your mother keeps you informed of Adam's movements?' She had never realised that, had simply believed Mark showed no interest in Adam, as she didn't.

Mark was still scowling. 'As you know, we're the only family he has, and with someone like Adam it's best to know exactly what he's up to!' He gave a rueful smile. 'A lot of good it did me this time,' he acknowledged in self-disgust. 'Look, like you've already said, it's been a long evening for you,' he said, before coming over and kissing her lightly on the cheek. 'The best thing is probably for us both to get that good night's sleep, and think about this again in the morning.'

Maggi didn't want to think about Adam at all; if she did she would never get to sleep! But she knew what Mark meant. Emotions were just running too high at the moment for any logic to be applied to the situation.

She smiled up at Mark gratefully. 'Don't forget to call Andrea,' she reminded him indulgently as he went to leave the room.

He paused to grin at her. 'Not unless I've ceased to value certain parts of my anatomy!' he conceded lightly, chuckling softly to himself as he left the bedroom.

Adam was so wrong about her own relationship with Mark; far from the two of them being lovers, Mark had developed a deep relationship with the woman who had been her physiotherapist for three years. Maggi was so pleased for them both; she liked Andrea enormously, and Mark more than deserved to find happiness.

Andrea was working in France at the moment, with a young child who had been involved in an accident, but she would be back in a few weeks, and in the meantime Mark was helping Maggi, taking care of all the details which she still found it something of a strain to deal with.

Three years... That was how long it had taken her to learn to walk again after the accident...

She and Adam had been coming back from a gig one night, both of them tired. Adam had been driving the powerful white Mercedes with his usual skill, but had been given no chance to avoid the other vehicle that had suddenly veered across the motorway onto their side of the road and hit them almost head-on. What had been so miraculous about it was that Adam had escaped almost unhurt, with just a few cuts and bruises, whereas Maggi had had a serious pelvic injury and had broken both her legs, giving the doctors serious doubts about her ability to ever walk again.

She had been in hospital for weeks, barely aware of her surroundings, let alone what was going on in the outside world. When she had left the hospital almost three months after the accident, it had been in a wheelchair.

But if she had thought there had been pain while she was in hospital it was as nothing compared to the misery she had suffered once she was at home. Life, as they said, had to go on, and what no one had told her, during those months when she was in hospital, was that Adam's life had certainly gone on—without her!

Such had been their popularity in those days that the two of them had been engaged to sing for months in advance, having bookings as far as eighteen months away. The performances they were to have fulfilled directly after the accident had been cancelled, but the ones following that hadn't been—and Adam had gone on to make them with someone else!

Maggi had met Sue Castle in the past, she and Adam having appeared together on the same bill as Sue a couple of times, but it had come as a complete shock to her to find that Adam was singing with the other woman, and very successfully too.

Of course, Adam had explained that it was only a

temporary arrangement, that once Maggi was back on her feet the present arrangement would be terminated. In the meantime Maggi had been left at home, battling to recover from the injuries that still made it impossible for her to walk, while Adam had disappeared night after night with the other woman. Until the night he hadn't come home…

Maggi gave a shudder of revulsion at the memory, standing up abruptly. Even now she didn't want to think about it, didn't want to remember that final humiliation. Adam hadn't replaced her in just the musical side of his life but in every way, leaving Maggi feeling totally superfluous, a useless waste of space and time as far as he was concerned.

But she wasn't superfluous now—not to herself, at least. She had spent her time building her life back up, putting the pieces back together. And she had succeeded; she had finally managed to walk again, to sing again, to resume her career. And if she knew part of her would never recover from Adam's betrayal perhaps that was a good thing too: she would never be so stupid about emotions and love ever again…

'I've ordered breakfast to be served in here,' Mark told her when she emerged from her bedroom into the lounge the next morning. 'I thought you would prefer it,' he added with a grimace.

As Mark had probably guessed, it hadn't been a good night. Her sleep, when she'd finally managed to drift off, had been filled with the nightmares that had once occurred with sickening regularity but which were now a rarity. At first, when she'd still been in hospital, the dreams had been about the accident, but later, once she was home again, those dreams had been about Adam—an Adam who seemed never to be at home, who always seemed distant and preoccupied when he was.

She smiled at Mark gratefully as she sat down to pour them both a cup of coffee. 'Good idea,' she said brightly, not wanting him to see just how disturbed a night she had really had. 'What are the plans for today?' She helped herself to some toast she didn't really want, lightly buttering it as she looked at Mark questioningly.

'I thought perhaps you should rest today—'

'But I rested yesterday, Mark. And the day before that,' she recalled ruefully. 'We haven't seen anything of the area yet,' she reminded him.

'The forecast is for rain today.' He frowned, drinking his own coffee.

'That shouldn't bother us too much in the car.' Maggi smiled. They had driven up several days ago in Maggi's BMW, deciding they would prefer the freedom of having their own transport during their stay; she was surprised Mark now seemed reluctant to take advantage of it. She looked at him closely. 'Has something happened, Mark?' He hadn't actually looked at her since she'd come into the room, and he seemed to be having trouble meeting her gaze now.

He looked startled. 'What do you mean?' he said sharply. 'What could have possibly happened? I told you, I just thought you might like breakfast in here.'

Maggi was more convinced than ever that there was something wrong; Mark was one of the most amiable, even-tempered people she knew, and yet at the moment he was definitely agitated about something.

There was only one person who was guaranteed to make him feel that way!

'Have you heard something else from Adam? Is that it?' she prompted ruefully. 'You really shouldn't let him get to you, Mark,' she dismissed, with more self-confidence than she actually felt; Adam had always been a force to be reckoned with. 'We—'

'I don't give a damn about Adam,' Mark told her as he stood up abruptly. 'Except that his mere presence here seems to create the usual problems.' He scowled darkly.

She shrugged. 'Maybe he's gone now; we certainly made ourselves more than clear last night!'

'I doubt it!' Mark grimaced. 'But it's really irrelevant now whether he's gone or not.' He gave an impatient shake of his head.

Maggi frowned up at him. 'Why now? Mark, what's happened?' She demanded to know this time, knowing that something certainly had.

He gave a heavy sigh. 'I was hoping you wouldn't have to know about this. I was going to shield you from it as best I could, but the situation seems to be spiralling out of control, and—'

'Mark, you still aren't making much sense.' Her frown deepened to one of puzzlement. 'If it isn't Adam, what situation are you talking about?'

'It isn't Adam himself, but of course he's involved in it. Up to his neck—as usual!' Mark's expression blackened. 'I've had to stop all telephone calls coming into the suite, and the hotel management delivered a message a short time ago to inform us that members of the Press are starting to arrive here at the hotel. They have managed to put the reporters off so far by claiming you aren't registered—which is basically true, because the suite is booked in my name.' He was talking almost to himself now. 'But I somehow doubt that's going to stop them for long—'

'Mark, what is this all about?' Maggi stood up too now, her agitation evident. He gave another heavy sigh, reaching down behind the sofa. 'A newspaper was delivered with breakfast. I took one look at it and sent down to Reception for the rest of this morning's publications. I wish to God I hadn't, because they just got progressively worse!' he groaned.

Maggi's hand shook slightly as she reached for the newspapers, the colour leaving her face as she saw the first headline. FENNELL AND CARMICHAEL REC-ONCILED IN MORE THAN MUSIC? She picked up an-other newspaper, swallowing hard at the more per-sonal leader of this one. MAGGI AND ADAM BACK TOGETHER? And the last one she looked at had her swaying on her feet. HAVE MAGGI AND ADAM SE-CRETLY RECONCILED?

Reconciled... Yes, she and Adam were still mar-ried, had made vows to each other in church—vows Adam had broken all too easily when it had suited him to do so.

There had been speculation about them in the Press for months after their separation three years ago, but it had eventually died down, leaving Maggi to apply quietly to Adam for a divorce. It was an application he'd chosen to ignore; the papers had never been re-turned to her, signed or otherwise.

Maggi had believed it best that they quietly break their ties with each other, but obviously this hadn't suited Adam at all. Perhaps his marriage to her had become a good safeguard against any other woman expecting a commitment from him! Whatever his reasons, she was still married to him.

Now the speculation about the two of them had begun all over again... Although she didn't think even Adam himself could have realised those repercussions that he had discussed would involve such personal speculation about the two of them. Or perhaps he had...? No, she was being ridiculous now. God, surely some part of her didn't still hope those nightmarish three years without Adam had all been just that—a nightmare? That would be madness itself!

CHAPTER FIVE

'WE HAVE to get out of here, Maggi,' Mark told her distractedly. 'The management aren't going to be able to hold them off for ever. I—' He broke off as a sharp knock sounded on the door. 'Oh, damn!' He suddenly looked as hunted as Maggi felt.

Understandably so. There was no back way out of this suite, and if the Press had—

'Open the damned door!' rasped an all too recognisable voice from the other side. 'Before someone sees me out here, puts two and two together—and comes up with five!'

'Adam!' Mark muttered. 'I should have known he wouldn't stay away.'

'I think we should open the door, Mark.' Maggi stood up. 'Adam's right. If he's seen—!' She moved swiftly to the door, unlocking it, moving sharply back as Adam instantly pushed his way into the room, closing the door firmly behind him.

He looked somehow older in the harsh light of day, flecks of grey more visible in the darkness of his hair, those lines Maggi had noticed the night before, beside his nose and mouth, more deeply grooved. He was thinner than he used to be as well, his denims resting low down on his hips, his pale blue shirt tucked in at the waistband. But his eyes were still the same, she noticed with shocked reaction, stepping back——cold and grey, like an arctic sea…

Those icy eyes took in the breakfast tray and the scattered newspapers before he turned his attention back to Maggi. 'You can't stay here—you do realise that?' he rasped harshly. 'If you do you'll become a prisoner in this suite, unable to—'

'And whose damned fault is that?' Mark attacked angrily, glaring at Adam. 'If you hadn't turned up in the way you did last night, none of this—'

'Give it a rest, Mark,' Adam advised wearily. 'Life is full of ifs, buts and maybes—and at the end of the day they don't make a damn bit of difference! The fact of the matter today is that the media are on the scent of what they think is a good story, and they aren't going to give up until they corner at least one of us.'

'So you thought you would just come here and add fuel to the fire!' Mark said disgustedly.

Adam looked at him contemptuously. 'Give me credit for a little sense! I—'

'I don't have to give you credit for anything, Adam,' Mark scorned. 'You're just a selfish bastard who—'

'I don't think this is helping the situation, Mark,' Maggi cut in gently, lightly touching his arm.

'It's a situation he created—'

'Mark.' She shook her head, her smile full of understanding for his anger; she was none too pleased by all this herself. But arguing amongst themselves wasn't going to help the situation. 'Mark and I were just about to leave,' she told Adam calmly.

'And just how did you intend doing that?' he returned scornfully. 'Members of the Press are swarming all over this hotel looking for your room even as we speak. The management have succeeded in holding them off so far—' he shrugged '—but it's really only a matter of time.' His mouth twisted. 'I suppose it's something to be grateful for that the two of you didn't register as Mr and Mrs Smith; that would have been a complete giveaway!' he added disgustedly. 'The name Forbes—' he looked pointedly at Mark '—is confusing them at the moment.'

Maggi looked at him angrily. 'We have no reason to book in as "Mr and Mrs Smith",' she told him contemptuously. 'We leave that sort of subterfuge to you!'

A nerve pulsed in Adam's rigidly clenched jaw, the only indication that he was holding back a caustic reply. 'Could we just cut the petty squabbling and get out of here?' he said impatiently. 'I have my car parked at the side entrance,' he continued before either of them could reply. 'And your departure has already been cleared with the management. If the truth be known, they will probably be pleased to see the back of you!'

Maggi could appreciate that this quiet, backwater hotel, albeit one of a larger chain worldwide, was far from used to having to deal with situations like the one that had been created here this morning. It would be much easier for the management if she and Mark really were no longer around. But to leave with Adam...!

'What do you mean "cleared with the management"...?' She frowned.

'I mean exactly what I say, Magdalena—cleared,' Adam bit out tersely. 'Now get your things together and let's go, before my car is discovered.'

He was right; there would be time once they were away from here to argue the point of paying their hotel bill. But argue it she would; she didn't want to be beholden to Adam for anything.

She moved to her bedroom without further comment, throwing the few things she had brought with her into her suitcase, hoping that Mark was doing the same, instead of squabbling with Adam. She couldn't hear any raised voices, so hopefully Mark was packing too.

'Separate bedrooms, hmm?' Adam remarked thoughtfully from the open doorway. 'Interesting...'

Maggi's face was flushed as she looked up at him. She hoped he would put it down to the exertion of packing, but wished, nonetheless, that Adam hadn't realised she and Mark were still just friends. If Mark wasn't the man in her life, then it would only lead to speculation on Adam's part as to who was...

'I've preferred to sleep alone since my accident,' she told him distantly. 'It's more comfortable for me.'

He raised dark brows. 'You mean the two of you make love and then Mark is banished to his own bedroom?' he enquired.

Maggi stiffened resentfully; she should have known he would jump to a conclusion like that. 'Our sleeping arrangements really are none of your business, Adam,' she snapped. 'You aren't here by invitation and have caused nothing but trouble since you got here. I certainly don't owe you any explanations.'

'You're my wife—'

'You were my husband, too,' she returned tautly. 'But you don't hear me asking you what you've been doing with your life since we parted. Or who you've been doing it with. Quite frankly, we don't have that much time,' she added tartly.

His mouth quirked. 'You never used to be bitchy, Magdalena,' he drawled.

Her face flushed anew. 'I never used to be a lot of things, but survival teaches you it's exactly that: survive or go under! Now, shall we get out of here? You seemed to think it was of the utmost urgency five minutes ago!'

'Leave the suitcase,' he instructed as she went to swing it to the ground in preparation for carrying it outside. 'I realise you're recovered, Magdalena, but I still doubt you're supposed to carry heavy things like cases.' He took the bag from her resisting fingers.

Maggi snatched her hand away as if she had been burnt, her skin tingling where it had briefly come into contact with his. Physically he had always had the strangest effect on her, right from the beginning, so much so that she had always melted at his slightest touch. She hadn't thought he would still have the same influence now, not after all that had happened between them...

He was right about the suitcase, though; she wasn't supposed to carry things that were too heavy. Her recovery had been nothing short of miraculous, and there was no way Maggi ever wanted to endanger that; she could still remember all too well how useless she had felt in her wheelchair. And how she had mourned all that she had lost. She was just starting to regain some of that, and had no intention of putting it at risk.

'Thank you,' she muttered with a distinct lack of

graciousness. Well, what did Adam expect? He was the last person she wanted to accept help from!

'You're welcome,' he returned. 'Do—?'

'Shall we get out of here?' A harassed-looking Mark stood in the doorway. 'One of the maids just came to the suite to say several of the reporters are on their way up!'

Maggi had been so caught up in her conversation with Adam that she hadn't even realised anyone had come to the suite. This was a mess—

'Just like old times!' Adam grinned, grabbing hold of Maggi's hand and pulling her towards the door.

She knew exactly what Adam meant. At the height of their popularity they had often had to escape from over-enthusiastic reporters, sometimes with hilarious results. But the whole point of resuming a solo career was that she didn't want it to be like old times; she had been trying to make a fresh start for herself. But Mark was right; there just wasn't the time right now to discuss any of these points. The important thing was to get away before any of the reporters saw them. Especially with Adam in tow!

And she could certainly do without Adam holding her hand!

There was a barely perceptible tightening of his fingers about hers as she tried to release herself, just enough pressure to prevent her escape. Maggi glared at him, pulling even harder to release her hand from his much larger one.

'Careful,' he warned softly as the three of them went out into the corridor. 'You'll hurt yourself.'

Hadn't she been hurt enough by this man? 'I can

manage on my own, Adam,' she told him through gritted teeth.

He didn't even turn to look at her, surveying the carpeted corridor to make sure they could still make their escape unmolested, then leading the way towards the side entrance where his car was parked. 'I'm sure you can,' he accepted dismissively. 'I happen to like holding your hand,' he announced with all of his old arrogance.

That just made Maggi want to pull away all the more, but by this time they had reached the fire-exit. They escaped outside, the coolness of the autumn air making Maggi wish she hadn't packed her jacket inside her suitcase along with the rest of her clothes.

'We'll be warm inside the car in a couple of minutes,' Adam reassured her smoothly.

Maggi looked up at him frowningly; how had he known she was feeling the cold?

He shrugged as he strode purposefully towards a black Range Rover. 'As I said last night, you always did like your creature comforts—and warmth was one of them!' He released her hand—finally!—to put down the suitcase and unlock the vehicle.

Maggi moved away gratefully, although she could still feel the imprint of his flesh against hers, clasping her two hands together in an effort to stop the tingling sensation.

'You get in the back, Mark,' he tersely told the other man as they stowed the two suitcases and Maggi's guitar in the boot of the car.

'I—'

'I don't want you cramped in the back.' Adam cut

in on her protest, going round to get in behind the wheel.

Maggi very much doubted that even Adam himself, for all his height, would be cramped in the back of his Range Rover. It appeared to have been built for luxury and comfort, the side windows tinted black, the seats made of beige leather. Adam reached over and pointedly opened the passenger door beside him, looking at her expectantly.

'Now isn't the time to dither, Maggi,' Mark advised. 'Let's just go and then we can sort out what we're going to do.'

He was right—she knew he was—but that still didn't stop part of her balking at the idea of Adam having his own way all the time. He always had in the past, and she had vowed that if they should ever meet again Adam would learn she was an individual, with a mind of her own.

'Get in the front, Mark,' she told him determinedly, moving around him to climb into the back, keeping her gaze firmly forward as she sensed Adam turning to look at her with amused grey eyes.

'You always were the stubbornest female I ever knew!' he muttered as he turned to switch on the ignition.

'Good to know some things don't change,' Maggi returned tartly.

Adam paused, turning to look at her. 'Actually, yes, it is,' he finally said huskily.

She swallowed hard, willing him to turn his attention back to driving, just wanting to get away from here and then Adam as quickly as possible. She certainly didn't want to have time to stop and think about what he could possibly have meant by that last remark! Whatever it was, she told herself, she wasn't interested.

'Can we just drive, Adam?' Mark was the one to prompt impatiently. 'Or do you intend to just sit here until the reporters find us?'

Adam didn't even bother to answer, putting the car into gear before accelerating away from the hotel.

Sitting in the back, Maggi had a chance to look at him unobserved. The last three years really hadn't dealt with him kindly. Those lines on his face were clearly evident in the bright light of day, as were the flecks of grey she'd already noticed in the darkness of his hair. He looked older than his thirty-eight years, appeared almost grim.

Perhaps life as a single man hadn't been as good for Adam as he had thought it would be. Maggi had avoided all knowledge of him during that time, hadn't wanted to deal with the possibility that he might be in a serious relationship, or test whether or not she was strong enough to cope with that knowledge. Sue Castle hadn't lasted long, Maggi did know that, but no doubt there had been a succession of women since Sue's departure from his life; Adam was not a man to be without female company for long. When had he ever been?

But Mark, it seemed, kept a closer watch on Adam's life, knew exactly what Adam was doing—although there was no way that Maggi would ever ask Mark *what* he knew!

She turned away abruptly. It was of no interest to her who Adam had in his private life. None at all! At least, she had thought it wasn't... For almost three years she had deliberately tried not to even think about Adam, not to imagine what he might be doing, but now, within a very short space of time, she suddenly found herself overwhelmed with curiosity.

Madness. Absolute madness. This man had almost destroyed her life once—she would not allow him to attempt it a second time!

'Where, exactly, are we going?' Her voice was sharper than she had intended, her thoughts filling her with impatience and tension.

'I'm staying in a friend's house in the area,' Adam answered with a shrug, without taking his attention off the road in front of him. 'I thought we could all go there for the time being while we decide what to do.'

A female friend? The question came unbidden into her mind. 'I'm sure Mark and I have no wish to impose upon your friend's hospitality,' she answered quickly. 'So—'

'I said I was staying in a friend's house, Magdalena,' Adam cut in dryly. 'I said nothing about the friend being there too. As it happens Geoffrey and his family are on holiday at the moment, and they offered me the use of their home while they were away.' He shrugged again. 'No problem.'

It might not be a problem to him, but Maggi certainly hadn't envisaged them continuing to spend time in his company. 'We merely need to devise a way for us to be able to pick up my car from the hotel,' she began firmly.

'You aren't going to be able to do that for several hours,' Adam answered reasonably. 'In the meantime we can all go and have a cup of coffee. Breakfast, too. I noticed hardly any of the food had been touched on your tray at the hotel.'

He noticed far too damned much as far as Maggi was concerned! He had made it his business to know she was performing at this folk festival. It would all have been so much easier if he hadn't.

'Maggi?' Mark turned to look at her concernedly.

What was she supposed to say? She would much rather not go anywhere near Adam's friend's house, or indeed Adam himself, but there was the problem of getting her car, and for the moment she was too confused by last night and Adam's presence now to be able to think straight.

'Coffee sounds fine,' she accepted tightly.

'And breakfast,' Adam put in firmly. 'You don't look as if you've been eating enough,' he added re-provingly, glancing in the driver's mirror at her thin, almost gaunt-looking face.

His concern for her welfare was way overdue. The time for his concern should have been three years ago, but of course then he had been more wrapped up in his career, and the woman who had briefly become his new singing partner. Maggi certainly didn't need his solicitude now!

'Toast and orange juice will be fine,' she assured him, meeting his gaze challengingly in the mirror for several friction-filled seconds before he had to turn away to return his attention to the road.

'Mark?' he prompted the other man tersely.

'The same,' Mark replied tautly. 'If it's not too much trouble,' he added with sarcasm.

'It was never too much trouble for Magdalena. One

of my favourite things used to be providing her with breakfast in bed,' Adam returned softly.

She could feel the heated colour flood her cheeks at what she knew was a deliberately provocative statement; the only 'breakfast in bed' she could ever remember Adam providing had never included food! But it had usually kept them in bed for a very long time...

He was trying to meet her gaze in the driver's mirror again, his eyes compelling—but Maggi refused to give him the satisfaction of letting him know she recalled all too well those 'breakfasts in bed'! How could she forget them? Their relationship had always been very physical, their responses to each other always instantaneous. Which was one of the reasons why Maggi was so unhappy with her reaction to Adam earlier...

She had thought, after all that he had done, that she couldn't possibly still want him. But there was no doubting that tingling sensation in her hand and arm after he had touched her. She only wished there were!

Mark glanced round at her. 'I'm sure the reporters will give up and go home once the management have told them we've booked out, so it should be easy enough to go back and get your car in a couple of hours.'

A couple of hours...! Spent in Adam's company? Oh, they were going to be a very long two hours!

'I really don't want to inconvenience Adam for that long. Perhaps you could drop us off somewhere?' Maggi suggested to him stiltedly.

'I'm not being inconvenienced,' Adam assured her dryly. 'And you've seen the newspapers; do you really think there is anywhere I could drop you off in this area those reporters wouldn't somehow get to know about and find you there?'

He had a point, and she for one did not want to fight her way through a barrage of questions from the Press. What a great choice—a couple of hours spent in Adam's company or having her privacy totally invaded!

'Strange,' Adam murmured. 'I have the distinct impression the two of you would rather not be here!'

'How astute of you.' Mark returned the sarcasm.

'Ungrateful pair,' the older man said dryly.

'Ungrateful—!' Mark repeated indignantly. 'If it weren't for you—'

'Yeah, yeah, Mark, I've heard it all before,' Adam dismissed wearily. 'Give it a rest, will you?'

He really was still the same arrogant Adam she remembered so well. Mark was right; he had created this situation for all of them, and now he was bored by it.

That was another part of Adam's personality she knew very well; he became bored very easily. She had spent months after their separation wondering if that was what had really gone wrong in their relationship, if Adam had become bored with her! In the end the reasons had become irrelevant; their marriage was over.

She had thought the happiest day of her life was the one when she'd married Adam, had imagined them spending the rest of their days together. Perhaps there was no such thing as a lifetime of love any more—although her parents seemed to have found it. They were still together after thirty years of marriage, and, she was sure, happy together. Maybe it was just that her own choice had been someone like Adam, a man too good-looking for his own—and every female's!—good.

She was back to looking for reasons again! At the end of the day—as she had finally realised after all her soul-searching—none of them mattered; it was over, had been over for a very long time.

'Here we are.' Adam turned the powerful vehicle down what looked to be a long drive; the house was not even in sight.

'Your friend likes his privacy,' Maggi remarked dryly after they had been driving for half a mile or so and the house had just come into view. It was an impressive Victorian mansion, with ivy crawling all over its red brick and the extensive surrounding gardens kept in immaculate condition.

'Actually his wife is the one who likes her privacy,' Adam answered as he parked the car on the gravel outside the front of the house. 'She's Celia Mayes, the actress.'

Maggi had seen the woman in numerous television programmes; she was a beautiful actress, making a name for herself in films at the moment, having been nominated for an Oscar for her last starring role. Tall and blonde, aged in her late twenties and with the sort of figure most other women would kill for, this seemed a strange location for her to choose to make her home.

'Geoffrey and Celia have twin boys, aged one, and they prefer to keep them away from the limelight,' Adam explained as he unlocked the door to let them all into the house.

It was difficult enough to imagine the other woman as a mother at all, with her exquisite appearance and perfectly proportioned body, but of twin baby boys…! How on earth did she manage to combine a marriage, children, and a career of the magnitude to which hers had grown?

'Geoffrey is the agent Geoffrey Haines?' Mark put in abruptly.

Adam looked at him with narrowed eyes. 'He's my agent, yes,' he nodded.

That was something new; in the past Adam had never wanted to bother with an agent. Still, he was a big star now, his work taking him all over the world, something it must be easier to organise with the help of an agent.

'And Celia Mayes',' Mark acknowledged hardly.

Adam looked at him again. 'Is that a problem?'

'For me? No,' Mark replied dismissively.

Grey eyes clashed with blue for several long seconds, and Maggi could feel the tension between the two men. She didn't understand it, but she could feel it. What on earth was going on now?

'This is a lovely house,' she said, more for something to say than anything else, although in truth it *was* lovely, having been furnished as a home rather than as a show-piece. Which was probably as well, with two very young children living in it!

'Yes, it is,' Adam acknowledged uninterestedly, leading the way through to the spacious kitchen at the back of the house. The oak panelling and cabinets had obviously been chosen with the age of the house in mind, the yellow and white colour scheme brightening the room up considerably. 'Sit yourselves down,' he invited, indicating the chairs at the oak kitchen table. 'I'll make us all a pot of coffee.'

Maggi sat down, relieved to do so. This was the weirdest situation! Here she was, sitting down, quite amicably, it seemed, having coffee and possibly breakfast with the man who had totally destroyed her life three years ago. Only the English could be this civilised.

'What are you smiling at?' Adam prompted indulgently.

She hadn't realised she was smiling until he pointed it out. But, yes, she supposed she *was* smiling, admittedly ruefully, but it was still a smile. Although it soon turned to a grimace. 'Life,' she said dryly.

He put mugs of freshly brewed coffee down on the table in front of them. 'The irony thereof?' he questioned wryly.

Trust him to know exactly what was so funny— and not necessarily humorously so!—about this situation. 'Something like that,' she replied, deliberately not looking at him as she sipped her coffee, although she could feel his gaze on her for several more, long, lingering seconds.

It really *was* all so civilised, and yet this man had betrayed her, hurt her, before finally walking out on her! She must never forget that. Never!

'Now, what have we got in here?' Adam was looking in the refrigerator, perusing its contents. 'Freshly squeezed orange juice for the lady.' He brought out a jug of the cooled liquid. 'Squeezed by my own fair hands this very morning,' he told her as he put the jug on the table with a flourish. 'And croissants.' He produced them from a bread bin on top of one of the units.

'I suppose you made those with your own fair hands this morning too?' Mark scorned.

Adam looked at him coldly. 'No, but I did collect them from the baker's and straight from the oven,' he answered curtly, getting butter and honey from the refrigerator while he warmed the croissants slightly in the microwave. 'Just the way Magdalena likes them,' he added huskily. 'I hope you like them too, Mark.' His tone gave the impression he really didn't give a damn whether his cousin liked croissants or not; that was what he was getting! Because that was what Maggi liked...

Fresh orange juice with warm croissants and honey—her absolutely favourite breakfast. And Adam had all the ingredients. Almost as if he had known she and Mark would be here for breakfast...

He had seen the reporters from the newspapers himself, would have realised how distressing their pursuit would be. But he couldn't possibly have known she and Mark would come and have breakfast with him. Could he...?

He was Adam; he *had* intended them to be here for breakfast—or it certainly seemed as if he had by the very fact that he was so prepared for their arrival. Wasn't the fact that they were here, against all the odds, proof of that?

She had suddenly lost her appetite, and slowly put down the croissant she had been in the middle of smearing with honey. 'I would like to use the bathroom,' she said stiffly, needing a few minutes' respite from the tension of this situation.

'Down the corridor, turn right, and— I'll show you,' Adam decided briskly, putting his own coffee down untouched.

Being alone with Adam was the last thing she wanted, either now or in the future, but she had made the statement about the bathroom; it would look cowardly to change her mind just because Adam had offered to direct her there personally.

'Thank you,' she accepted abruptly, shooting Mark a resigned look.

He gave her a reassuring smile as she left the room, trailing behind Adam. What else could Mark do? What could either of them do other than accept the situation they found themselves in at the moment? Later, once they were away from here and had their own transport back, it would be a different matter entirely!

'Don't look so apprehensive,' Adam turned to remark dryly. 'I'm not about to try and ravish you on the bathroom carpet—comfortable as I'm sure it would be!' He pushed open the bathroom door, revealing that the white carpet had a thick, deep pile, luxurious to the feet—and the rest of the body!

Deep colour darkened her cheeks at the erotic thoughts that briefly ran through her head at his provocative remark. What was she doing?

'Thank you,' she muttered dismissively as she entered the room, willing him to go away.

But that was something he seemed reluctant to do, now that he had finally got her on her own. 'For what?' he taunted. 'Not ravishing you on the bathroom carpet? Or showing you where the bathroom is?' He quirked mocking brows at her.

'The latter, of course,' she snapped irritably. 'I mean both!' she amended impatiently as she saw his grin and realised exactly what she had said; she had made it sound as if she wanted him to make love to her on the bathroom carpet!

Adam looked down at her with indulgent humour. 'Make your mind up, Magdalena,' he drawled softly. 'Mark probably wouldn't come looking for us for a while...'

He was being ridiculous, and he knew he was, but he was obviously enjoying tormenting her. 'I made my mind up about you a long time ago, Adam,' she snapped waspishly. 'Go and find someone else to flirt with; it's wasted on me!' She closed the bathroom door in his face, firmly pushing the lock across into place, breathing deeply as she waited for the sound of his retreating footsteps from the other side of the door.

They were a long time coming, but finally she heard him moving back down the corridor towards the kitchen, and started to breathe easily again, herself once more. What a nightmare these last few days had been—an absolute nightmare. The sooner they left here the better. Perhaps then she could resume a normal life. Well...as normal as it could be since Adam had invaded it.

She took her time freshening up, renewing her lip-gloss and blusher, brushing the length of her hair down her spine. The deep blue blouse she wore was almost a perfect match for her eyes and her fitted denims emphasised the slenderness of her hips and thighs.

She didn't give the appearance of someone having to get through one of the most traumatic experiences in her life to date—being this close to the man she had once loved to distraction. Which was good, because she didn't want him to realise just what an effect he was having on her. Wouldn't Adam just love to know the havoc he was wreaking on her already strained nerves?

She had no trouble finding her way back to the kitchen—mainly because she only needed to follow the sound of raised male voices to know exactly where she was going; Adam and Mark were arguing yet again. The two men, after her initial break-up with Mark, had never really been friends, but as members of the same family they had been polite to each other, at least.

Not any more, though; their voices were getting louder than ever as Maggi approached the kitchen.

'You have no idea what you're talking about, Mark,' Adam was saying coldly.

'Everyone—except Maggi, it seems!—knows what I'm talking about,' Mark returned scornfully. 'You and Celia Mayes!'

Maggi shrank back against the wall of the hallway, her face paling. What on earth—?

'The rumours have been flying thick and fast about the two of you over the last couple of years,' Mark continued contemptuously. 'And lo and behold here you are, staying in Celia Mayes' home!'

'It's Geoffrey's home too,' Adam pointed out icily. 'And he would hardly invite a man be believed to be his wife's lover to move into his home for several days!'

'It's a well-known fact that Geoffrey Haines is absolutely besotted by his beautiful wife; he would probably give her anything she asked for!' Mark scorned.

'Including making a friend of her lover?' Adam derided harshly. 'You're talking rubbish, Mark, and you know it.'

'Do I?' the younger man challenged.

'I really don't give a damn whether you do or not,' Adam dismissed. 'I'm just warning you against repeating those rumours to Magdalena.'

Magdalena had just heard them...

CHAPTER SIX

'I STILL think you're making a mistake,' Adam muttered grimly. His teasing banter of earlier had gone completely in the face of Maggi's stubbornness.

He was driving Maggi and Mark back to the hotel, at Maggi's insistence, protesting all the way—as only Adam could protest!

Maggi had taken several minutes out in the hallway to recover from the shock of Mark's accusations about Adam and Celia Mayes. She didn't know why she was so shocked, really; there was no difference between Adam having an affair while he was married and him having an affair with a woman who was married to someone else. It was still adultery—and Adam was good at that!

It had come as a devastating blow to her three years ago to realise that Adam wasn't just singing with Sue Castle but having an affair with her too. And that it might have been far from the first time in their relationship it had happened. Adam was a man who liked to live by his own rules, and whilst the one of fidelity in their marriage applied to Maggi it didn't necessarily apply to Adam himself. In fact, it definitely hadn't!

But the fact that he was now endangering other people's marriages—especially that of a woman with two young children!—by his own lack of morals was absolutely disgusting as far as Maggi was concerned, and the sooner she got away from him, and Celia's house, the better. Adam had been far from pleased when she'd returned to the kitchen and told him she wanted to leave, although he'd given in when she remained adamant.

'It's far too early for you to go back and get your car,' Adam bit out impatiently during the drive back. 'I rang the hotel before we left, and the place is still crawling with reporters.'

Maggi didn't care. Being bombarded with a barrage of unwanted questions was better than having to spend any more time with Adam. He hadn't changed. He never would...

'Magdalena—'

'The name is Maggi, Adam,' she cut in harshly. 'Maggi Fennell. It always has been; it always will be.' She looked at him challengingly, having elected to sit in the front of the Range Rover beside him, so disappointed in him she didn't care where she sat this time.

It was ridiculous, she knew, to let him affect her like this after all this time. But it was very difficult, when she was in his company, to block out all of the past; after all, they'd had some good times together. If they hadn't, the bad ones wouldn't have caused her so much pain!

But how badly she had misjudged him, and the love she'd thought they felt for each other. Adam was an owner, a possessor, but he had no intention of ever giving *himself* one hundred per cent.

'Not to me,' he ground out forcefully. 'Never just Maggi to me!'

'I think what Maggi is trying to tell you,' Mark put

in from the back of the vehicle, 'is that what you have to say on the subject is of little importance to her!'

If she was honest what Adam had to say on any subject was of little importance to her! But she could see how Mark had enjoyed baiting the other man, thought how sad it was that two cousins should have such a dislike of each other. Because of her, she readily acknowledged, but nevertheless it was still sad. As an only child, of parents who were also only children, she had always found it such a waste when relatives didn't seem to get on together, had always wanted a huge family of her own. That would never happen now...

'You know something, Mark,' Adam replied in a voice so soft it was menacing. 'You're even more of a pain now than you were years ago!'

'Coming from you, I'll take that as a compliment,' Mark returned unconcernedly.

Maggi had to smile, turning away. At least Mark was no longer bothered by Adam's arrogance. Probably because he knew their time in his company was so limited; they should reach the hotel in a few minutes.

'Magdalena—'

'Thank you for the orange juice and coffee, Adam,' she cut in dismissively, having had no appetite for croissants when she had eventually returned to the kitchen. 'I'm sure the two of us have appreciated your help this morning.'

'Now go away?' he said dryly.

She turned to look at him unflinchingly. 'Exactly!'

'That might be a little difficult,' he returned. 'We

have a performance this evening,' he reminded her, eyebrows raised.

'No way!' Mark was the one to answer him. 'Maggi goes on alone, or not at all.'

'Everyone is going to be expecting—'

'What?' Mark interjected heatedly. 'The two of you together? I don't think so.' He shook his head. 'Maggi is singing in a small nightclub this evening; there just wouldn't be room for the crowd the two of you would attract. The organisers of the festival will just have to announce your personal non-appearance before the performance.'

Oh, great! So that no one was disappointed it would have to be explained before she sang that Adam was not going to perform with her this evening! Maggi Fennell on her own, take it or leave it! Wonderful!

If the organisers had any sense at all they would accept a decision by her not to sing; no matter what was announced, the audience would be expecting Adam to make a surprise entrance.

Knowing Adam as she did, they wouldn't be the only ones! She certainly wouldn't trust him not to be at the nightclub this evening. She interrupted the men's argument. 'I have no intention of appearing this evening.'

Adam looked at her sharply, his mouth twisted derisively. 'Chickening out again, Magdalena?' he taunted harshly. 'It seems to be a habit of yours,' he added contemptuously.

She had never chickened out of anything in her life! How dared he say such a thing? He—

'You don't know what the hell you're talking

about.' Mark was the one to answer him heatedly. 'Maggi has more guts than you'll ever have. She—'

'I don't believe I addressed the remark to you, Mark,' Adam returned icily. 'I was talking to Magdalena.'

She was totally stunned by his attack, totally agreed with Mark's outrage; how dared he talk to her like that? If he knew the pain she had suffered in the last three years in an effort to walk again... But Adam had no idea what she had gone through—because he hadn't been there! He had never been there for her.

'I don't have anything to add to Mark's comment,' she told him frostily. 'I have no intention of defending myself to you.'

'But you don't intend singing tonight?' His mouth was tight with disapproval.

'No,' she answered abruptly.

'Where is your professionalism?'

'It's still firmly in place, Adam,' she bit out. 'The fact that I carried on last night more than proved that!' All she had wanted to do was run when he'd come on stage with her! But she hadn't; she had stayed where she was and braved out the situation. And those stories in the newspapers this morning were the price she had paid for that bit of bravado! 'Though I don't have anything to prove to you, Adam, or to anyone else,' she added tightly. 'And I have no intention of repeating last night's performance.'

'You—'

'The subject is not up for discussion, Adam,' she told him adamantly. 'I'm withdrawing from the festival.'

'As I said,' he muttered, 'you're chickening out.'

He was being deliberately provocative now, and Maggi waved Mark to silence as he would have risen to the bait; she didn't intend giving Adam the satisfaction. What did his opinion matter anyway? She had proved to herself what needed proving at this festival, and she could go on from there. The thing to do now was to distance herself—and her career—as far away from Adam as possible.

As Adam had predicted, there were still a lot of reporters milling about the reception area of the hotel. But as Adam had paid their hotel bill for them—something Maggi intended rectifying at the earliest opportunity!—there was no reason for them to actually go inside.

'My car is over there,' she directed Adam abruptly, pointing out her black BMW to him.

He looked at the reporters with narrow-eyed assessment. 'We may just get your luggage into your car before they realise it's us,' he conceded grudgingly, swinging his Range Rover over towards her car.

How it must have pained him, after all his dire warnings to the contrary, to have to admit that! But the change-over of luggage was made with the minimum of effort by the two men once Adam had parked the Range Rover next to Maggi's car, and the reporters were barely aware of them before they had got into their respective cars and driven back out of the car park.

'He's following us,' Maggi muttered minutes later to Mark, having spied the Range Rover behind them in her mirror almost as soon as they'd turned onto the main road. Adam continued to follow them even though it was in the opposite direction to the house where he was staying. 'Damn!' she muttered again as Adam flashed the lights of his powerful vehicle, obviously wanting her to stop now that they were well away from the hotel and there were no members of the Press around.

Mark glanced round in time to see Adam flash the lights again. 'Just ignore him.' He turned back to Maggi. 'We don't have anything more to say to him.'

'He isn't going to give up, Mark,' Maggi sighed a few minutes later when the Range Rover showed no sign of dropping back, despite their own obvious lack of intention of stopping.

'He never did,' Mark muttered grimly.

Maggi wasn't altogether sure she agreed with him on that; Adam had certainly given up on their marriage when the going got too tough.

'Okay, we had better stop,' Mark conceded heavily. 'But I'll be the one to go and talk to him.' He straightened in his seat, ready to get out of the car once Maggi had pulled over to the side of the road.

But, before Mark could even undo his seat belt, it seemed, Adam was out of the Range Rover and standing beside Maggi, obviously waiting for her to open the car window so that he could talk to her. Something she did with great reluctance...

'We haven't forgotten about the hotel bill, Adam.' Mark was the one to speak to him. 'The money will be forwarded on to you! I didn't realise you were so short of money, or I would have reimbursed you earlier.'

Adam gave the younger man a contemptuous look, the only indication he gave that he had heard Mark at all, before turning his attention on Maggi. 'I'll be in touch,' he told her huskily.

It was the last thing she wanted to hear, although she couldn't have said it was altogether unexpected. 'You stopped me just to tell me that?' She looked at him impatiently.

'We didn't exactly get the chance to say goodbye.' And before Maggi could take in what he meant, let alone take evasive action, he had leaned forward, bent his head and lightly brushed his lips over hers. Her immediate instinct was to gasp, and even as she did so she could feel him deepening the kiss, his mouth moving searchingly against hers.

'For God's sake…!' Mark muttered incredulously. 'What the hell—! Adam, stop that!' he ordered frantically.

Adam had no intention of stopping anything, and it was left to Maggi—who was mortified at her own brief response!—to be the one to wrench away.

She was breathing deeply in agitation as Adam slowly straightened up away from the car, his own expression one of grim satisfaction. He knew that she had responded to him too.

'That felt more like hello,' he said seductively, grey gaze assessing.

She knew exactly what it had felt like, could still feel the tingling pressure of his mouth moving against hers. How dared he do that to her? How dared he humiliate her in front of Mark in that way? Or perhaps that was why he had done such a thing in front of his cousin; despite their two bedrooms at the hotel, Adam still didn't seem convinced that she and Mark weren't lovers.

'Goodbye, Adam.' Her voice was low as she pressed a button to close the window next to her. She put the car into gear, not caring whether he had stepped back from the car or not, and accelerated away, not even sparing him a glance in the driver's mirror.

'Bastard,' Mark muttered at her side.

She had to agree with him. Adam hadn't had to behave in that cavalier fashion. But then, Adam being Adam, she supposed he had...

She was devastated that she had responded. It wasn't good enough that she had been taken by surprise, that she hadn't believed even Adam was capable of such audacity; Adam was capable of anything, and she should have been the first person to realise that.

But to have kissed her...

Why had he done such a thing? What on earth could he hope to gain by it? Except hurting her once more, of course...

'It's the record company again,' her mother told Maggi with a pensive frown.

Maggi had lived back at home with her parents for the last three years because she hadn't been able to cope on her own after the accident—and not just physically. Her parents had been a great source of support to her during her recuperation, but they were all at a loss now to know how to deal with this new and constant pressure from the recording company for her to make another album with Adam.

It was the publicity from the festival that had caused this, of course; subsequently, the record company had re-released one of their old CDs, while at the same time clamouring for a new one to follow its undoubted success. A request Maggi had adamantly refused twice already during the last two weeks since her return from the festival.

'Shall I tell them again that you're unavailable?' Her mother looked at her questioningly.

That reply had worked twice, but she doubted it would work a third time. The problem, as far as she could see, was that Adam had already consented to do the album, which increased the pressure on her to agree to it also.

Adam's behaviour just didn't make any sense to her. It hadn't at the festival and it certainly didn't now, and she had no intention of being in the kind of close contact with him that making an album together would bring. She had told him she intended to sing alone, and that was the way it was going to remain.

But how to get the record company to accept that? That was the problem... Especially as she had hoped, with the renewed interest in her career, to be able to bring out an album of her own in the near future.

'I'll take the call, Mamá, thanks.' She got wearily to her feet, taking the receiver from her mother. She was a woman of almost fifty and the likeness between the two of them was unmistakable, although her mother kept her dark hair styled shoulder-length, and her eyes were dark brown rather than the blue Maggi had inherited from her father.

'You don't have to do anything you don't want to do, Maggi; remember that.' Her mother squeezed her arm reassuringly before leaving her to take the call in private.

'You don't have to,' agreed an all too familiar voice as she put the receiver up to her ear, and she almost dropped it in her agitation as she instantly recognised the caller. 'But you would be a fool not to do this, Magdalena,' Adam added dryly.

She gathered her wits together quickly, knowing he was hoping to disconcert her—and he certainly had!—but unwilling to give him the satisfaction of knowing he'd succeeded. 'I wasn't aware you were into owning recording studios, Adam,' she returned dismissively. 'But my answer is still no.'

'I'm not; I merely offered to talk to you personally as you seem to be proving so difficult. Your refusal isn't a good career move, Magdalena,' he reasoned tautly.

'For whom, Adam?' she taunted. 'My career is going exactly as I want it to, so I can only presume you're the one in need of the extra publicity.'

She had done a couple more gigs in the last two weeks, both of them very successful indeed. Admittedly they would have been even more so if Adam had been there, and the audience had initially called out for him, but once they'd realised she was genuinely alone, her reception couldn't have been warmer. But there had been two more red roses...

'Maybe it's your career that needs the boost, Adam...?' she added softly.

'I wouldn't pay too much attention to Mark, if I were you,' he came back scornfully. 'His remarks tend to be biased, to say the least. And where is my dear cousin on this bright and sunny day?' he added derisively. 'Out getting you more engagements like the festival?'

That festival had been deliberately chosen for her first public appearance in three years, after much debate and discussion within her family as well as with Mark. Despite Adam's mockery—and his unexpected appearance there!—it had been a good choice. As for Mark, he was spending some time with Andrea now that she was back from France. Although that was none of Adam's business either.

Unlike Mark's interest where Adam was concerned, Adam didn't seem to have taken any interest in Mark's life over the last three years. Otherwise he would have known about Andrea. But Maggi had no intention of enlightening him about Mark's relationship with her. She had no intention of telling him anything.

'Adam, I have given the record company my answer.' She ignored his remarks about Mark. 'And I'm giving you the same answer—'

'Let's have lunch and talk about it,' he cut in determinedly.

'Let's not have lunch and let's not talk about it,' she came back quickly, no longer amazed by his audacity; he was just more outrageously arrogant than she remembered. 'Goodbye, Adam.' She rang off before he could come back with anything else.

She hadn't questioned why Adam had been negotiating with the record company in the first place; she didn't want to know, didn't want to know *anything* about him. But he had been entering her life with sickening regularity over the last few weeks, after years of not hearing anything from him at all. Perhaps, she admitted, she just hadn't been emotionally strong enough in the beginning to be told what Adam was doing with his life—or whom he was sharing it with!—and, now she was, most people seemed to have realised it was a subject best left alone.

Was Celia Mayes the woman in his life at the moment? It seemed a strange arrangement if she were. But then, when had Adam's life ever been straightforward?

'Everything all right?' Her mother put her head tentatively around the door.

Maggi stood up determinedly. 'Couldn't be better,' she answered brightly, deciding it was probably best not to mention what Adam had said in their telephone conversation; her parents felt pretty much as Mark did about him.

Her mother looked relieved as she came fully into the room. 'The sooner you get an album of your own together the better.' She nodded.

The problem with that was that while the recording company were pressuring her to make an album with Adam they were reluctant to listen to any request she made to record one of her own. And as she was still technically contracted to them...

But it wouldn't always be like that. Once the publicity from their joint appearance died down, she had no doubt that the recording company would see the sense in having a solo album out rather than nothing at all. And she had written enough songs now to put that album together.

It was strange... Adam had always been the songwriter in their partnership, but during the last three years, with lots of time on her hands, Maggi had managed to write twenty songs herself. Even to her critical eye they looked good. She was quietly confident that the recording company would recognise that too. In time...

In the meantime she intended forgetting about her telephone conversation with Adam. No one could make her do anything any more, and especially not with Adam!

Gardening had always been a great escape for her, letting her mind just drift while she concentrated on the task at hand, and, while they were into autumn now, there was still a lot of tidying up to do in the flowerbeds, ready for winter. Gardening had been one of the things she'd missed the most after her accident, and as soon as she was mobile again she had started to spend hours outside in quiet solitude, healing herself inside as well as out.

Her parents' dog, Arthur, a long-haired collie, leapt and bounded about the garden as Maggi concentrated on weeding. It would save her father, a busy doctor, having to do the work at the weekend.

Strangely, she had spent a lot of time working in the garden in the last two weeks. Since her return from the music festival...

'Hello there, Arthur,' greeted a smooth male voice. 'As full of energy as ever, I see.' Adam laughed throatily as the dog leapt up and down in front of him.

Maggi was in the middle of weeding under the apple tree when she first heard his voice. Sitting back on her heels now, she was aware that her hair had been whipped into a tangled black mane by the briskness of the wind, that her face was completely bare of make-up, that her denims were old and faded, her checked shirt even more disreputable, and that her hands were black with dirt from her exertions in the flowerbeds over the last hour.

An hour during which Adam had obviously used his time to drive down here. Well, he could damn well turn his car around and return to London!

CHAPTER SEVEN

'YOUR mother is in the kitchen and didn't see me arrive,' Adam told her as he saw her worried glance towards the house. 'I saw you out here in the garden when I arrived, and so I—'

'Just walked in,' Maggi finished accusingly, putting down her small rake to wipe her hands down denims already slightly smeared with earth. 'With your usual arrogance!' Her eyes flashed angrily. 'When will you ever learn that you aren't wanted?'

'Where you're concerned?' Grey eyes were narrowed ominously. 'Probably never.' He shrugged.

Now, what did he mean by that? Adam had never been the most straightforward of men, and— She was doing it again! She mustn't care what he meant, mustn't have any interest in anything he had to say.

'You aren't welcome at my parents' home, Adam,' she told him bluntly. Her parents were as unforgiving where this man was concerned as she was. Which wasn't surprising. The man who should have stood by her three years ago had let her down in the worst way possible, leaving her parents to pick up the shattered pieces. No, he wouldn't be welcomed there. By any of them.

'I realise that.' He nodded abruptly. 'But I also know they've always had your best interests at heart.'

'If you're back to the subject of the two of us recording an album together,' she bit out scornfully as she stood up, 'then I can assure you they don't think that is in my "best interests" any more than I do!' The opposite in fact; her father had threatened to punch Adam on the nose if he came near her again.

Which would be a feat in itself! She had acquired her lack of stature from both her parents, and her father was only five feet six inches high; he would need to stand on a box to be able to reach Adam's aristocratic nose!

Thinking of which, she glanced at the watch on her slender wrist; her father should be back for lunch after his morning surgery at any moment. Although the thought of her father standing on a box in order to punch this man was quite amusing, she wanted it to remain just that—a thought. There had been too much bitterness already, without involving her parents any further.

'You have to go, Adam,' she told him coldly.

He shifted slightly, his stance suddenly implacable. 'I'll go when I'm good and ready,' he announced arrogantly.

He looked so vitally male, standing there with the breeze lightly ruffling the darkness of his hair, a black jacket worn over a white shirt and faded denims. A flicker of awareness shivered down her spine—a shiver she instantly suppressed.

'Fine. You do that.' She bent and picked up her tools, intending to return them to the shed on her way back into the house. 'Just make sure you close the gate after you as you leave; Arthur still doesn't have any road sense.' She turned and walked away.

'Magdalena!'

'Goodbye, Adam.' She didn't even turn to look at

him, her strides purposeful now, but not in the least hurried; the last thing she wanted was to look as if she was running away.

'You really do walk very well again.'

He spoke softly, but loud enough for her to hear! Maggi spun sharply on her heel, her face white with outrage now. How dared he even mention that? How dared he? She had been like a broken doll when he'd betrayed her, unable to walk, unable to sing, unable ever to have— How dared he?

A sob caught in her throat, whether of pain or anger she wasn't sure. All she knew was that at this particular moment in time she hated this man. Hated this man she had once loved most in all the world...

'Steady.' He had reached her side, his hands clasping her arms as she swayed, almost toppling over. 'I didn't mean to startle you.' His expression was grim, his gaze concerned on her ashen face. 'I only—'

'Go away, Adam,' she told him in a flatly controlled voice, firmly extracting herself from his grasp. 'Go away. And don't ever come back,' she bit out vehemently.

'Magdalena, it's been three years—'

'Don't tell me how long it's been!' She spat the words out at him, her eyes flashing blue fire. 'I'm the one who's had to live through those years, trying to walk again, to sing again, to put my life back together.' She was breathing hard in her agitation now, angry in part at her own physical weakness.

If only she hadn't lost her balance—but she did occasionally, probably always would, the specialist had told her. But she had done so much better than anyone had expected. Than this man had expected. A crippled wife was certainly something he had never envisaged. Or, indeed, accepted. Well, she wasn't crippled any longer, not by physical disability, and she didn't intend this man to cripple her emotionally either.

He gave a pained frown. 'Isn't it time to forgive—?'

'And forget?' she finished contemptuously. 'I don't ever want to forget, Adam. Not what you were then. And who you are now.'

'You don't know who I am now, Magdalena.' His voice was huskily soft. 'I've suffered too the last three years—'

'Your conscience finally caught up with you?' she derided hardly, glaring at him. 'Well, don't look to me for forgiveness, Adam. Because I can't give it to you.' And she couldn't. Not after what she had lost, what he had taken from her. Certainly she couldn't forget this man's wanton destruction. That was completely unforgivable.

He frowned down at her, grey eyes dark. 'You never used to be bitter, Magdal—'

'Don't try and lay a guilt trip on me, Adam,' she cut in with a scornful laugh. 'You were always very good at turning the tables so that everyone else came out in the wrong and you remained free of blame. Only this time the evidence is too damning, Adam. Too final,' she added.

He recoiled as if she had actually hit him, his expression bleak. 'I lost something too, Magdalena,' he bit out tautly. 'Something all of you seem to conveniently forget.'

Tears filled her eyes—tears she rapidly tried to

blink away. 'As easily as you forgot your marriage vows. Now—'

'I didn't forget my marriage vows, Magdalena,' he ground out fiercely.

'Misplaced them, then,' she scorned. 'The result was the same. You—'

'Maggi, Ted—when are the two of you coming indoors for your—?' Her mother broke off her gentle chiding as she rounded the corner of the house and saw the two of them in the garden, and her face suddenly stilled. 'I heard voices... I thought it was your father teasing you again about pulling up the flowers and leaving in the weeds...' She absently mentioned the long-standing joke between father and daughter.

Maggi had started to help her father in the garden when she was quite young, but the first time she had decided to weed the garden for him, when she was about eight, she had unwittingly pulled up all his tenderly nurtured flowers and left all the weeds in the ground. It was something he had never let her forget!

'Adam,' her mother grated now, brown eyes cold.

'Maria,' he returned curtly. 'You're looking well.'

Her mother did look well; she had the sort of beauty that only seemed to deepen as she grew older. Although at the moment she lacked her usual warm smile and was frowning darkly at Adam.

'I don't know why you're here, Adam—although judging from the telephone calls we've had this last couple of weeks I can probably take a good guess!' she added before he could make a reply. 'But, whatever your reason, I would like you to leave now. You're obviously upsetting Maggi.' She looked pointedly at the two bright spots of angry colour in her daughter's cheeks. 'And I know Ted will be far from pleased to see you too. He hasn't been too well recently...' She let slip her concern for her husband's health.

'I'm sorry to hear that,' Adam returned smoothly. 'Nothing serious, I hope?'

'Just the usual stress and strain attached to being a family doctor,' Maggi's mother dismissed briskly. 'But I don't want him worried.'

Maggi knew that her own ill health, the strain it had placed on all the family, hadn't helped. She was an only child, and her parents had felt her pain as much as their own. The last three years hadn't been easy for any of them...

'I think I hear your father's car now, Maggi,' her mother said anxiously, turning back towards the house. 'Please go, Adam,' she entreated, pausing briefly before going back inside.

'The feeling appears to be unanimous,' Adam said with dry self-derision.

Maggi's eyes flashed deeply blue as she turned back to him. 'What else did you expect?'

He shrugged broad shoulders. 'I've never been a vote-of-the-majority man; it doesn't allow for individualism.'

In other words, he had no intention of going anywhere until he was good and ready—and at the moment he appeared to be neither of those things!   But, if anything, her mother had made light of the condition of her father's health; he had actually collapsed in his surgery a week or so ago, shortly after Maggi had returned from the music festival, and now had a locum helping him out until he was fit enough to take over his practice duties fully once again. He really didn't need the added stress of seeing Adam.

'*Please* go, Adam.' No doubt her father would have seen the Range Rover parked somewhere outside in the street, but as he had no idea Adam had such a vehicle he wouldn't make any connection between the two.

'I want to talk to you,' Adam told her determinedly. 'If not here,' he added, as she would have protested, 'then somewhere else. I noticed a little coffee shop in the town as I drove through earlier; we could go there.' His eyes were narrowed as he waited for her answer.

Maggi's brows rose. 'Adam Carmichael in the local coffee shop!'

He continued to look at her steadily, not amused by her mockery. 'I drink coffee like everyone else,' he rasped. 'I'll see you there in fifteen minutes.' He turned on his heel and strode forcefully across the garden, letting himself out the way he had come in, by the side gate.

Maggi frowned at his sudden departure, knowing she would have to meet him; if she didn't, he would come back. And both her mother and her father had endured enough stress and strain over the last three years to last them a lifetime.

Her father was in the kitchen drinking tea when she entered the house a few minutes later, a short, sandy-haired man, tending towards plumpness in middle age. Although, of late, his face had started to take on a certain gauntness...

'Been digging up the flowers again, I hear,' he

greeted her, with a smile, absently patting the dog's head as Arthur bounded over to greet him.

Maggi smiled, accepting the teasing. 'I think I may have left a few bulbs in for next spring. I'll leave the two of you to have lunch alone; I need to pop into town for a few things.' She had seen the way her mother had glanced anxiously past her as she entered the room, and knew she was looking for Adam, so now she was doing her best to reassure her that he had gone. But he hadn't gone very far... 'Can I get either of you anything?' she offered as she picked up her handbag and car keys.

'We're fine,' her mother answered. 'Don't you think you should change those clothes first?'

Her denims and shirt looked a little the worse for her morning in the garden, but she had no intention of looking as if she had changed to go and meet Adam. 'I shouldn't be long.' She shook her head.

'Well, at least wash that smudge of dirt off the side of your nose and brush the earth off your jeans,' her father suggested dryly.

Great. She had spent the whole of the time talking to Adam with dirt on her nose! 'I'll do that.' She nodded. 'And no whisking Mamá up to bed for one of your siestas,' she joked, none of them ever having forgotten the time when she was a child and had returned early from Sunday school because the vicar wasn't feeling well, only to find her parents cuddled up in bed together, obviously post-lovemaking; they had been as startled to see her as she'd been to see them there. 'I'll only be an hour or so,' she warned her father as she stood at the kitchen sink, drying her face after washing away the dirt.

'At my age, Maggi, an hour is more than long enough!' he returned self-derisively.

'We're embarrassing Mamá,' Maggi realised indulgently as her mother blushed. 'But...' She paused on her way out of the door. 'I never did believe that story you gave me about thinking of adopting Abuela and Abuelo's tradition of the siesta!'

Her father grinned. 'I always did say you were a bright child. Too bright for your own good sometimes!' he added with mock reproof.

Maggi laughed to herself as she left the house, but it was laughter that faded as soon as she had unlocked her car and begun the drive to meet Adam. She didn't like the fact that she had been pressurised into this meeting.

Lowell was a small place, boasting only one coffee shop—a local woman's attempt at introducing a little gentility to the small farming town. Its chairs and tables were made out of pine, green and white cloths were spread over the latter, and several pastels adorned the walls, with greenery in every other available space.

Adam looked totally incongruous seated amongst the coffee shop's tweeness; he was the only man in the room and his frame looked too large for the pine chair with its green and white checked cushion.

He looked up as she came in, obviously relieved at her arrival. The place was fairly full with women who had been shopping this morning and were now taking a break for their lunch. Most were keeping a surreptitious eye on the man in their midst, obviously having recognised him as someone they knew, although so far none of them seemed to have been brave enough to approach him and confirm his identity. Otherwise Adam wouldn't still be sitting there! As it was, the occupants of the surrounding tables were talking animatedly together in whispers.

They recognised Maggi too as she entered. Several of them were her father's patients, but even the people that weren't knew her as the doctor's daughter. Unfortunately, after the recent publicity in the newspapers, several of them recognised her as Adam's wife too now!

'I ordered us coffee,' he muttered as she joined him at his table. 'I didn't order you any lunch; I'm not sure what you eat any more.' He scowled.

He hadn't seemed to have any trouble choosing her breakfast a couple of weeks ago!

'Not a lot, by the look of you,' he added tersely as he looked at her closely. 'You're too thin, Magdalena.'

She bit back her caustic reply as two coffees were brought to the table by Sally, who was the proprietress as well as the waitress.

Maggi could see the other woman's eyes widen as Sally saw who had joined her prestigious customer, knew that speculation in the town would be rife over the next few days. In which case, someone was sure to mention it to her father on a visit to his surgery, negating the whole purpose of talking to Adam away from the house!

'That wasn't a criticism, Magdalena.' Adam had noted her frown—and misinterpreted it. 'Merely an observation.'

As if what he had to say about the way she looked was of any importance to her!

'Duly noted, Adam,' she dismissed, adding sugar to her coffee. 'But I would prefer not to order lunch, thank you.'

'Not intending to stay long enough to eat it, hmm?' he guessed.

She certainly wasn't—had no intention of eating a cosy little meal with him. The food would probably stick in her throat, anyway! 'I've told the record company and I've told you. I will not—'

'Damn the record company!' he cut in forcefully, eyes glittering fiercely as he hunched forward across the table, bringing his face dangerously close to hers. 'This isn't about the two of us making a record together, and you know it!'

'Do I?' She studiously avoided the curious glances of the other people in the coffee shop—a coffee shop that seemed to be rapidly filling up. And Maggi could guess why. News, good or bad, travelled fast in a small community like Lowell. Despite her mockery of Adam's coming here earlier, she knew he was the reason for this sudden need for coffees and light lunches by the locals.

'Magdalena—'

'Don't!' She physically recoiled as he would have put his hand over hers as it rested on the table. 'I—'

'Would you like to have lunch now?' Sally stood beside their table, waiting to take their order.

Adam looked up with a warm smile. 'Is it all right for us to take up one of your tables just to drink coffee during your busy lunchtime?'

'Of course.' Sally responded coyly to his warm charm, putting her order book away in her overall pocket. 'Take your time.'

'As smooth as ever, I see, Adam,' Maggi remarked dryly once the other woman had left them.

He shot her a glacial look. 'It costs nothing to be polite to people, Magdalena,' he reproved her harshly.

She gave him a scathing look. 'I wonder if you would have been as "polite" if it had been a man wanting to take your order?'

He bit back his own sharp retort with effort, breathing deeply. 'I'm not going to get into an argument with you, Magdalena,' he told her. 'Mainly because I realise that's exactly what you want me to do.'

Of course it was what she wanted! She wanted the chance to heap accusations on him because she hadn't had the opportunity to do so three years ago, wanted to tell him of all the anger she had felt towards him that night he hadn't come home—the night he had spent in another woman's arms, the night their marriage had ended for ever... Because she hadn't said anything to him then, and she hadn't seen him since that day she had sent him away, and it had been burning inside her unspoken for long enough. Of course she wanted to get into an argument with him!

'I'm not about to waste my breath on lost causes,' she dismissed coldly, however. 'And you were always that.'

'I'm your husband!' he bit out.

'You were never that.' Her expression was bleak.

'We were married for two years—'

'*I* was married for two years,' she corrected him vehemently. 'You were still Adam Carmichael, stud extraordinaire!'

His hand gripped her wrist painfully, too strong to

be pushed away this time. 'Don't start believing all
the drivel you've read about me—'

'I didn't need to read about it, Adam, I lived it!'
Her eyes were deeply blue in her vehemence. 'And
would you let go of my arm, Adam?' She looked
down to where he held her. 'People are staring.'

'I don't give a damn—'

'About anyone else's feelings but your own,' she
finished scornfully. 'But then, you never did. But I
do. And I'm the one who has to live here. So if you
wouldn't mind removing your hand?' She continued
to look pointedly to where his fingers still encircled
the slenderness of her wrist.

Instead of releasing her he tightened his grip, his
thumb lightly caressing the place where her pulse
could be felt racing. 'I always liked touching you,
Magdalena.' His voice was huskily soft now.

And she had always liked him to do so, had always,
in the past, been ready, melting to his touch.

She was ashamed to realise today was no different…!

The memories flooded back with torturous insistence: the two of them naked together, their bodies
entwined as they lay in bed, nothing between them
then, her hair entwined—deliberately so by Adam—
about his neck and chest, his hands touching her, caressing her, in places and ways that no one else had
ever done, every part of her crying out with need, with
a deep burning that she knew Adam would slowly and
pleasurably assuage.

Oh, God, never to know his kisses again, his caresses. Never to know that total oneness—

She stood up suddenly, wrenching her arm out of

his hand, doing it easily as she caught him unawares. 'I have to go, Adam,' she told him breathlessly, her cheeks pale. 'I didn't want to be here in the first place. I only came—well, you know why I came.' She couldn't even look at him, didn't dare do so at that moment. She hadn't broken down for so long—and she refused to now, in front of Adam. 'I have to go,' she repeated flatly, turning on her heel and leaving the coffee shop.

Her car was parked in the square across the road, but it seemed as if it was miles away, her legs feeling like leaden weights. Andrea had said she would continue to have good days and not so good days—and this was definitely not a good one!

She wasn't even sure she was going to make it to the car, a film of perspiration breaking out on her brow, dampening her fringe as she struggled to make every difficult step.

She flinched as she felt the strength of Adam's arm coming about her waist, fingers tightly gripping her as he held her protectively against his side and they crossed the road together.

'Can you make it?' Adam looked down at her contorted face. 'Or do you want me to carry you?'

Carry her? She would get to her car under her own steam if she had to crawl there on her hands and knees. This man hadn't been around when she had needed someone to lean on physically, and she wouldn't let him help her now.

'I can do it,' she told him between gritted teeth. 'Let go of me,' she ordered, relieved that they were on the square at last.

'You'll fall if I—'

'Believe me, I won't!' she assured him, inwardly

praying she wouldn't do exactly that if he released her. To find herself grovelling on the pavement at his feet would be just too much to bear. As it was she was fighting back the tears of frustration; she had never wanted to show weakness of any kind in front of this man ever again.

Adam studied the dogged determination on her face before slowly releasing her.

To her everlasting relief she didn't fall. She swayed a little, and her head still felt slightly dizzy, but she didn't fall.

'There.' She smiled up at him triumphantly. 'I told you I could do it.'

His expression was still grim. 'I thought, because you had returned to your career, that you were completely better,' he rasped.

Her mouth tightened. 'Compared with the helplessness of being confined to a wheelchair, this *is* better!' To be able to walk again, to drive, do all the things she used to do, if not quite as quickly, was tantamount to a miracle to her.

'But I thought—'

'What did you think, Adam?' she challenged scornfully. 'That the doctors had patched me up so that I would be as good as new? That I was the singing, walking Maggi Fennell once again?' She shook her head, an expression of disgust on her face as she looked up at him. 'Is that why you finally came back into my life, Adam? Because you thought, with my return to singing, that everything was back as it had once been?'

'I thought your appearance at the music festival

meant you were at least physically fit again,' he conceded slowly.

'And just what did that mean to you, Adam?' She could feel her strength slowly returning as they stood engaged in this verbal battle of wills, knew that when they parted she would be able to walk the short distance to her car. 'Did you think it would be as if the last three years had never happened? That if nothing else we could resume singing together—now that I'm physically fit again!' Her voice rose sharply in her agitation.

'As usual, you're simplifying things, Magdalena—'

'As usual, you're prevaricating, Adam!' she scorned. 'Adam Carmichael's unwritten rule: never directly answer a question, just in case you incriminate yourself. Well, for the last three years I've been working towards the fitness I have now. I have no idea what you've been doing for that time—and, quite frankly, I have no wish to know,' she told him quickly as he would have spoken. 'Your life, and what you do with it, is of no interest to me whatsoever.'

She had deliberately not thought about him, hadn't wanted to torture herself with thoughts of who he was with now. But for the last two weeks that hadn't been as easy; she knew who he was involved with at the moment. Just thinking about him and the beautiful actress together, the beautiful actress with her twin sons, was enough to rip Maggi apart inside.

No, she didn't want to know about his life, not if she were to remain sane...!

'Is it of any interest to you what *I've* been doing with my life for those same three years, Adam—'

'No!' he cut in harshly

'Why not?' she derided bitterly. 'Can't you bear to hear about—'

'No, I can't bear to hear!' He spoke fiercely, a nerve pulsing in his tightly clenched jaw.

'Why is that?' she taunted. 'Don't tell me you have a heart after all, Adam?' She shook her head. 'That would take rather a lot of readjusting to!'

'Of course I have a heart, damn it,' he rasped. 'I've loved you—'

'And left me,' she finished derisively. 'No, that's not quite right,' she said thoughtfully. 'You were never truly with me in the first place!'

He gave a deep sigh and closed his eyes briefly and regretfully. 'That isn't true, and you know it. I loved you, lived my life for you. Things only changed between us after the accident—'

'Of course they changed!' Her voice rose angrily once again. 'I couldn't walk!'

'I didn't mean—'

'I had two broken legs and a broken pelvis,' she reminded him emotionally. 'I could no longer be with you, sing with you. Be a proper wife to you!' She choked over the last words, knowing how easily Adam had found someone else to be in his life who could fulfil all those roles for him.

And how much, at the time, she had just wanted Adam to hold her...

It had been difficult, she accepted, during the months spent in hospital until her bones mended, and then the following weeks and months at home, to have anyone so much as get close to her without causing her pain. But it didn't mean that during all of that time she hadn't wanted Adam near her, hadn't ached for his touch and to be able to touch and make love to him in return. How she had yearned for those things, to feel like a woman again in his arms, to shut out all the pain and think only of how much they loved each other, to know that nothing else mattered.

But Adam had stayed away from her, had been off working a lot of the time. He certainly hadn't ached to touch her as she had ached for him—had found someone else to assuage any aches of that kind he might have had.

'That isn't what I meant either, damn it,' Adam snapped. 'Stop twisting my words, Magdalena. Things changed after the accident because I couldn't get near you any more—'

'I was in hospital, Adam, surrounded by doctors and nurses.'

'Once upon a time there could have been a hundred doctors, and the same number of nurses, and it wouldn't have mattered to us.' His eyes glittered furiously. 'I couldn't get through to you any more, couldn't reach you. You had shut me out,' he remembered. 'Just the sight of me seemed to make you more ill.'

'That isn't true…' She frowned at the thought of him feeling that way. Those first few weeks in hospital were mainly a blur to her, filled with pain and loss, utter despair. At times she had almost wished she had died rather than have sustained such horrific injuries. When she had learnt of Adam's betrayal, she *had* wanted to die.

'I'm telling you it is,' he bit out forcefully. 'I could feel your resentment towards me every time I came to the hospital to see you.'

'Was that any reason for you to—? Resentment?' she echoed. 'I never felt resentment towards you, Adam.' A lot of other emotions, yes: fear of losing him, pain at not being with him, love—a love she hadn't felt was returned by that time—hate at what she finally knew to be his betrayal of everything she had thought they meant to each other, despair at all they had lost. But resentment? No, she was sure she had never felt that emotion where Adam was concerned. 'Never,' she repeated with certainty.

He watched her with narrowed eyes. 'Not even for the accident?' he said slowly.

She shook her head, her hair, long and silky, swaying around her waist. 'I never blamed you for the accident. The police said there was nothing you could have done. Those boys in the other car were drunk— there was nothing you could have done to avoid the collision when the driver lost control of his car and crossed the central reservation. I never even considered that the accident could have been your fault,' she denied firmly.

'But what happened afterwards?' he rasped.

What happened afterwards? What did—?

She turned away, no longer able to look at him, knowing her inner pain would be reflected in her eyes and not wanting Adam to see that. He hadn't been there at the time to share that pain; he certainly wasn't going to see it now!

'I have to get back, Adam,' she told him stiltedly. 'I told my parents I would only be an hour or so—'

'You're twenty-six years old, woman, surely not answerable to anyone any more!' he said contemptuously. 'We're in the middle of a conversation that, in my opinion, should have taken place three years ago!'

'You weren't there to have this conversation with!' she returned coldly. 'The oh, so busy Adam Carmichael. You're right, Adam; I'm not answerable to anyone—least of all you! I—'

'Why haven't you and Mark ever married?' he continued determinedly. 'Is it because, as I suspect, you lost the baby, and any more children are out of the question?'

If she had felt weak crossing the road minutes ago she now felt as if she might collapse completely. No one, no one *ever* mentioned the baby any more. She had been five months pregnant at the time of the accident, had just reached that stage in pregnancy when her normal clothes no longer fitted her, had felt the baby's fluttering movements inside her, had begun to look at nursery furniture, to wander indulgently through baby-clothes shops.

And then nothing. No more little movements inside her, no more waking up in the middle of the night because she was so excited at the prospect of having Adam's baby she couldn't sleep, no more wondering if their child would be a son or a daughter.

He had been a son, a tiny, perfect little boy, but too small to possibly stand a chance of life when Maggi had gone into premature labour right after the accident that night three years ago. Her internal injuries had meant that in all probability there would never be another baby.

But no one talked about that any more...!

Least of all Adam. Adam, who had been with her

when their son had died. And who had never really been with her again.

'You're wrong, Adam.' Her eyes sparkled as she looked up at him, with a mixture of anger and unshed tears. 'Mark and I have never married because I'm unfortunately still married to you!'

She hoped Mark and Andrea would forgive her the lie. At the moment she just wanted to hurt Adam as she had been hurt, time and again. She knew her friendship with Mark was a weapon that could still do that, had known it at the music festival when Adam had come to the hotel.

'But that can all be changed now. Expect to hear from my lawyer, Adam,' she told him finally. 'I want a divorce, and I want it now!' She turned and walked off, no longer weak, filled with the strength of her hate towards this man.

'When hell freezes over.' The anger in Adam's softly spoken reply carried his words across the car park to her.

Maggi didn't so much as falter as she strode towards her car. After Adam had ignored her request for a divorce two years ago, she had decided that it wasn't important anyway, that she didn't need it. But she wanted it now, wanted to be completely free of this man. Once and for all.

Her last view, as she drove out of the car park, was of a gushing middle-aged woman obviously asking him for his autograph...

CHAPTER EIGHT

'MAGGI, love, what's going on?'

She looked up, her gaze slightly unfocused on her father where he stood just inside the dining-room. She was sitting slightly back from the table, her guitar on her knees, music spread out on the table-top in front of her.

As in the past, music was her salvation when she wanted to escape from the here and now. Ever since her conversation in the car park yesterday with Adam, she had wanted to do just that!

The only thing she had actually done where Adam was concerned was contact her lawyer and tell him to send off a second set of divorce papers. Via the record company if he couldn't contact Adam in any other way. Hell *had* frozen over as far as she was concerned!

She smiled at her father now as she gave him her full attention. 'It wasn't that bad, was it? The song,' she explained as he looked as blank as she had seconds ago.

He shook his head, no answering smile on his lips. 'Maggi, have you seen the newspaper this morning?' He frowned.

'It hadn't been delivered when I came in here. Perhaps Mamá—'

'I'm not looking for the newspaper, Maggi,' her

father cut in sharply. 'I know where it is. And, like everyone else, I'm curious as to what is going on.'

Maggi sat forward as she slowly put her guitar down on the table, her eyes unwavering on the paleness of her father's face. On closer inspection he looked strained, a grey tinge to his cheeks. The newspaper appeared to be the answer... 'I haven't seen it,' she said slowly.

'Then perhaps you should,' he told her heavily. 'I'll go and get it for you—'

'No, I'll come through,' she said abruptly, standing up, running her hands down her denim-clad thighs—hands that suddenly felt damp. She had a terrible feeling...!

That feeling was borne out as soon as she looked at the front page of the newspaper. There were two photographs there, both of them of Adam and herself. 'Before' and 'After', they had been captioned. It was obvious, after looking at the photographs, exactly what 'before' and 'after' the newspaper was showing!

The first photograph portrayed herself and Adam sitting in the coffee shop, smiling. Quite when it had happened during that awful conversation, Maggi couldn't imagine; she didn't remember smiling at Adam at all! Then she realised, as she looked more closely at the photograph, that they weren't actually smiling at each other but at someone not in the picture. Whoever had taken this photograph had been very clever; the picture of their happiness together in each other's company was completely misleading. The two of them were smiling at Sally as they apologised to her for not ordering any lunch!

The 'after' photograph was much more truthful

about the whole encounter; Maggi was striding away from Adam in the town square, dark hair flowing, mouth tight, and Adam was some distance behind her, a look of fury on his face. No chance of hell freezing over with the mixture of fiery emotions obviously crackling in the air between them!

Maggi glanced at her parents as they sat at the kitchen table. Their expressions were anxious, her mother's more so—because she knew of Adam's visit here yesterday—a visit that they had both decided not to bother Maggi's father with.

But some clever photographer had taken care of that for them!

Maggi couldn't even begin to imagine how it had happened, hadn't been aware of anyone in the vicinity taking photographs of them, and didn't know how the photographer could possibly have known about the meeting in the first place. She hadn't known about it herself until Adam had arrived here so unexpectedly. Adam... Could he possibly be responsible for this...? He was capable of anything; she knew that better than anyone. But setting her up like this...?

'Maggi?'

She looked up at her father anxiously, paying attention to him with effort. 'I have no idea how anyone managed to take these photographs.' Although, secretly, she had a pretty good idea!

'Oh, Maggi, it isn't the taking of them that's important,' her father sighed. 'I just—I don't—Adam's back, isn't he?' he said dully. 'After everything you said about him.' He frowned. 'I don't understand what's going on.'

'Nothing is going on! Adam is not back!' Maggi

cried heatedly. 'Not in any way that's important, anyway,' she added impatiently. 'He's making a nuisance of himself, as these two photographs show only too well.' She threw the newspaper down in disgust. 'But it's a nine-day wonder, a game Adam will soon tire of. We all know what a low boredom threshold he has,' she added bitterly. 'And when this game becomes too much of a bore for him he will just disappear again!'

'Calm down, Maggi,' her father soothed gently. 'I was merely thinking out loud just now, wondering why Adam has chosen now to come back into your life...'

She shrugged. 'It seems to be because of this album he wants us to make together. Other than that, his motives are as much a mystery to me as they are to you. As usual!' she added derisively.

Her father raised his eyebrows in bewilderment. 'Well, he really seems to have opened up a hornets' nest this time. Mark has already been on the telephone this morning. Apparently, as your agent, he has been inundated with calls from newspapers and television programmes, all of them wanting an exclusive interview with you. Don't worry,' her father reassured her as she looked alarmed. 'Mark has taken care of all that. All I'm saying is, things could be a bit awkward around here for a while.'

That proved to be the understatement of the day! The telephone began to ring even as her father issued his warning, the caller a reporter, and it continued to ring almost continuously for the next hour, until wanting a brief respite, her father took it off the hook.

But when her father attempted to go to his surgery

a short time later it was to find a large group of reporters waiting at the bottom of the pathway, ready
to pounce on anyone trying to leave or enter the
house!

To Maggi's relief, Dr. Fennell finally managed to
fight his way through to his car and make good his
escape. He checked later in the morning to see if the
reporters were still there—which they were, despite
repeated requests from Maggi for them to go away!—
and decided he wouldn't bother coming back for
lunch.

Not that Maggi could blame him; she was starting
to feel like a prisoner in her own home! Her only
consoling thought was that Adam was probably suffering the same fate. Probably more so; his popularity
had only increased over the last three years during his
solo career, whereas she had faded into the back-
ground.

Mark arrived as Maggi and her mother were eating
a salad lunch, groaning as he walked into the kitchen
and saw them both. 'Normality in the face of adversity, hmm?' he teased, bending to kiss Maggi's
mother lightly on the cheek in greeting. 'No, I won't,
thanks.' He refused her offer to join them. 'But you
two carry on eating and I'll make us all a cup of tea.'
He moved about the room with the familiarity of years
of friendship.

Maggi watched him as she continued to eat. There
was a suppressed excitement about him, an air of
something she couldn't quite place. No doubt Mark
would tell her when and if he was ready...

One thing she had learnt from the last three years

was patience. In the circumstances, she had had no choice!

'I think I'll take my tea upstairs and lie down,' her mother said apologetically once they had cleared the remains of their salad away. 'A siesta seems like a good idea today,' she added with feeling.

'Well?' Maggi prompted once she and Mark were alone.

'Amongst others, the record company rang me this morning,' he answered her, not even attempting to prevaricate. 'They've come up with a new offer.'

Maggi had rung the record company on her return from the coffee shop yesterday, telling them that any further negotiations would have to be done through Mark; she had no intention of having to deal personally with another visit from Adam! Nevertheless, she was surprised at the promptness of this offer...

'What is it?' she asked warily.

'They've agreed to you recording and releasing an album of your own songs—'

'They have?' she leapt in excitedly; maybe Adam had done her a favour yesterday after all! 'But this is great! When do I—?'

'Your own songs, Maggi,' Mark repeated firmly, holding her gaze with his own, 'but accompanied by Adam.'

Her excitement left her and she felt like a deflated balloon. A catch, there was always a catch, and it was invariably Adam...

'Don't dismiss the idea out of hand, Maggi,' Mark encouraged as he easily read her disappointment. 'The main thing is they have agreed to you making an album of your own songs—'

'With Adam!' She shook her head in refusal as she spoke. 'No way, Mark. Never!' She gave an inward shudder. Sing her songs with Adam? Share all the emotions with him that had compelled her to write the songs in the first place? No—she could never work that closely with him again.

'You're unknown as a songwriter, Maggi,' Mark reasoned. 'Adam has agreed to sing them unseen.'

'I wonder why?' she grated.

'For all anyone knows, your songs could be rubbish.'

'You and I know that they aren't!' she defended indignantly.

'All I'm saying is—'

'I know what you're saying, Mark—and the answer is still no! Contracts don't last for ever.'

'But for the moment it's binding.'

'I would rather never make another record than sing with Adam again,' she stated vehemently. 'And, quite frankly, I'm surprised at your about-face on this,' she accused him.

Mark sighed. 'I haven't done an about-face. I'm just—'

'Putting Adam's point of view!'

'No, not Adam's, the record company's,' he insisted. 'It may be the best offer we can get.'

'No,' she told him adamantly. She still felt exactly the same: to work with Adam, be that intimately involved with him again, go through all the emotions of her songs with him, and the reasons she had written each and every one of them? No, she couldn't do it!

Mark shrugged at her stubbornness. 'We may not get another offer.'

'Then we leave it. I'll just carry on doing my gigs wherever I'm wanted. I'll sing my songs then. I don't care, Mark,' she said firmly as he would have protested again. 'It's my way or not at all. I've worked too hard, Mark, been through too much, to let Adam ruin this for me now. I—' She broke off as the doorbell rang. 'Reporters.' She wrinkled her nose with distaste. 'They'll wake Mamá up if they carry on like that,' she added irritably as the doorbell shrilled again.

'I'll get it,' Mark told her. 'I'll just tell them to go away—nicely!'

Maggi shared a smile with him before he left to answer the door, although the smile faded as soon as Mark had gone out of the room. It was Adam's fault the reporters were camping on her doorstep. It was Adam's fault the record company wouldn't consider her as a solo artist. It was Adam's fault—

'It's Adam!'

The statement so coincided with her thoughts that it took Maggi several seconds to realise exactly what Mark was saying!

But as she took in the darkly powerful figure standing behind Mark in the doorway she realised he meant exactly what he had said—it was Adam. Larger than life, his expression grim.

She gathered her thoughts together quickly, her mouth twisting derisively. 'Come to view your handiwork, Adam?' she challenged.

Mark winced. 'Maggi—'

'I haven't come to "view" anything.' The fierceness of Adam's voice matched his expression, as he moved past the other man to enter the kitchen. 'I—'

'Don't tell me today's fiasco isn't your doing,'

Maggi dismissed. 'Where did you have the photographer hidden yesterday, Adam? It was all rather clever—'

'Magdalena, I haven't come here to listen to fanciful accusations, either,' he interrupted. 'Your father is in hospital with a suspected heart attack, and you—'

'Daddy is?' she cut in anxiously. 'I don't know what you mean.' She rubbed her forehead dazedly. 'How could you possibly know—'

'Your father came to see me earlier.' Adam answered her question abruptly. 'While we were—talking, he collapsed with pains in his chest. Being a doctor, he knew exactly what was happening to him. I drove him to hospital and he's there now, undergoing tests to see if it was a full-blown heart attack or a serious case of angina. He wanted me to come here and assure you and your mother that he's okay, before the two of you rush off to the hospital in a panic!'

Maggi was having trouble taking all of this in. She didn't understand what her father had been doing going to see Adam—how he even knew where Adam lived now, because she certainly didn't! And she didn't know what the two men could possibly have found to talk about. She did understand that her father was seriously ill in hospital. And that she would have to go upstairs and tell her mother...

Dear Lord, what was happening to them all?

'I'll go and talk to Maria,' Mark said gently. 'No offence, Maggi, but I think your mother would only have to take one look at the whiteness of your face for her to become hysterical. I think it might sound better—if something like this possibly can—' he gri-maced '—coming from an outsider.'

She nodded. For Adam to break the bad news was obviously out of the question! Having a conversation with him seemed to have already caused the collapse of one of her parents; she couldn't risk him blundering in and upsetting her mother too! The mere sight of him, after the morning they had all had, would prob-ably be enough to do that, anyway.

'You get yourself ready, Maggi.' Mark touched her arm encouragingly. 'I won't be long.'

She was sure he wouldn't; once her mother heard the news about her father she would be down here raring to go.

As for herself, she couldn't think what she needed to be ready. A jacket? Yes, probably. Her handbag? Yes, she would need that too. What else—?

'He's going to be all right, Magdalena,' Adam told her huskily, grey eyes dark with emotion.

She had been trying to block Adam out of her con-scious thoughts. It seemed that every time she so much as turned around lately he was there. But she didn't want to think about that now; she had to con-centrate on her father. 'Good,' she returned abruptly.

'About what you said earlier, regarding a photog-rapher. I had nothing to do—'

'Not now, Adam,' she dismissed agitatedly. 'Which hospital did you take my father to?' It suddenly oc-curred to her that it might not be the local one, ten miles away, because her father had gone to see Adam.

He shrugged. 'I told you, he realised what was hap-pening to him and insisted on going to Melchester.'

Then he was quite near to them. And she hoped Adam was right when he said it wasn't serious.

'I'm driving you there, Magdalena,' Adam said abruptly. 'You and your mother. Mark can follow in his own car, if he cares to, but I promised your father I would be the one to drive the two of you to see him.' He added those last words almost challengingly.

Maggi couldn't be bothered to argue with him. What did it matter who drove them to the hospital, as long as they got there? Their lives had been in turmoil again since Adam had come back, and all she wanted at the moment was to see her father and reassure her mother and herself that he really was okay.

Her mother was very pale when she came downstairs a few minutes later, but seemed strong when Maggi moved forward to hug her. She remained controlled in the Range Rover, keeping up a politely distant conversation with Adam as she sat beside him in the front of the vehicle on the drive to the hospital. In all honesty, Maggi was amazed at her mother's calmness, but accepted it was probably the only way she could deal with the terrible shock she had just received.

However, that calm deserted her mother completely once they were taken to Intensive Care to see Maggi's father. He lay so still in the bed, attached to several monitors, looking nothing at all like the lively, dependable man he usually was.

Her mother burst forth into a stream of emotional Spanish, speaking too fast for any of them to understand, before she launched herself into her husband's arms.

Maggi could clearly understand the reason for this

break in control; her father suddenly looked very old, and the gaunt look that had haunted his face in the last few weeks was even more pronounced. Maggi felt like bursting into tears herself!

'Let's go and talk to the doctor.' Adam took a firm hold of her arm, guiding her out of the room. 'Butt out, Mark.' His grip tightened on Maggi's arm as the other man stood outside the hospital room, having been refused entry because he wasn't immediate family. 'If you want to make yourself useful then go and see if you can find coffee for all of us!'

Mark looked as if he was about to explode at being ordered about in this way, but one look at the strain on Maggi's face and he bit back the angry retort he had been about to make to Adam. 'I'll be right here when you need me, Maggi.' He squeezed her shoulder reassuringly.

'She won't need you,' Adam rasped harshly. 'Coffee?' he prompted Mark pointedly as he made no effort to move away from Maggi.

Mark shot Adam another furious look, but Maggi couldn't be bothered with their petty quarrels just now. All she wanted was to know her father was going to be all right!

But she was no nearer knowing that even once they had spoken to the doctor in charge of her father; there were far too many ifs and buts in the conversation for Maggi's liking. The next twenty-four hours were critical. There would be further monitoring for several days. He needed no stress, no worries, complete rest. Then tests. And then more tests. More rest. And then finally he might be allowed home into their care. As long as he continued to rest, with no stress, no strain, no worries…

Maggi felt the last instruction was completely unnecessary. Of course none of them wanted to cause her father any worry. It was totally nonsensical as far as Maggi was concerned for the doctor to even think it necessary to issue such a warning to a doctor's daughter! What did this man—?

'Thank you, Dr Stokes.' Adam was the one to conclude the meeting, shaking the other man by the hand before leading Maggi out of the room. 'He's only doing his job, Magdalena,' he said gently once they were outside in the corridor. 'Painting the scenario, offering advice. As he would with anyone in the same circumstances.'

She gave a heavy sigh, closing her eyes briefly. 'I suppose so. I just— It's—it's just so—awful,' she admitted shakily.

'I understand.' Adam nodded. 'I do know how it feels to have the life of someone you love hanging in the balance,' he added gruffly. She looked at him uncomprehendingly. 'I'm talking about you, Magdalena!' he told her impatiently when she still looked puzzled.

Her? But— 'I don't think that is relevant, Adam,' she finally bit out in denial, her cheeks flushed. 'That's the past; this is now,' she told him agitatedly.

He gave a brief nod of acknowledgement. 'But the past is always relevant to here and now. I don't—'

'Oh, Mamá!' Maggi cried as her mother came out of her father's room, rushing to her side. The two women hugged in their mutual despair.

'He's all right, Maggi,' her mother assured her

huskily, attempting a smile that didn't quite reach fruition. 'He wants to talk to you. And Adam,' she added pointedly, drawing Maggi's attention to the fact that Adam had once again moved protectively to her side.

And Adam...? Why on earth did her father want Adam there? *She* didn't want him there!

'Your father isn't to be upset, Magdalena,' Adam reminded her quietly, obviously able to read the rebellion in her expression.

She was well aware of that fact—but surely seeing Adam was likely to cause upset? Wasn't it talking to Adam that had put her father in here in the first place?

'Ah, here's Mark with the coffee.' Adam spoke briskly. 'Magdalena and I are going in to see Ted now, Mark. Take care of Maria.'

Mark looked as startled by this turn of events as Maggi felt, grimacing as he put down the tray containing the plastic cups of coffee. 'Oh, but—'

'Just do it, Mark,' the other man told him sharply. 'You're here to help, not add to the chaos!'

Maggi felt sorry for Mark, knew he must be absolutely furious at Adam's treatment of him. But at the moment she couldn't help him. She just wanted to see her father. With or without Adam!

She was grateful for the fact she had grown up a doctor's daughter, otherwise the presence of the monitoring machines would have been more terrifying for her than it actually was. Although the situation was bad enough! Her father was only fifty-three; it was awful that something like this should have happened to him. She couldn't get it out of her head that he had been talking to Adam when it had occurred...

Her father was still very pale but he looked a little

brighter as Maggi approached the bed, his smile warm as he looked up at her.

'Rather a dramatic way to get a holiday,' he told her with self-derision.

'Oh, Daddy!' She gave a choked laugh at his attempt at humour, tears flooding her eyes.

'Now don't you go getting all emotional on me too.' He spoke firmly. 'Your mother has already made my chest all soggy and waterlogged!'

She blinked back her tears, knowing he was right; one of them had to remain strong. Her parents had been there for her for such a long time... 'Personally I think you're just trying to get out of all that end-of-summer gardening,' she said dryly.

'Probably.' He smiled his relief that she wasn't about to weep all over him too. 'Adam.' He turned his head. 'I'm sure you know why I wanted to talk to both of you.'

'Leave it for now, Ted,' Adam told him gruffly.

Her father shook his head. 'It's been left too long already. I don't—'

'I'm afraid you will have to leave now.' The nurse who had been standing so unobtrusively at the back of the room spoke to them softly. 'Mr Fennell is becoming agitated,' she explained with a rueful glance at the monitors.

Her patient glared at her fiercely. 'I'm not agitated, young lady,' he snapped. 'I wish to speak to my daughter and her husband—'

'Perhaps later,' the nurse soothed, looking pleadingly at Maggi and Adam, asking for their co-operation as the lines on the monitors began to dip and swell in an irregular pattern.

'I am a doctor, young lady—'

'Then you should know she is just doing her job,' Adam told him firmly. 'Magdalena and I can come back another time.'

'But I need to talk to Maggi—'

'You have a lifetime to talk to Magdalena,' Adam said. 'And I'm not going anywhere either,' he added. 'We'll both come back when you're a little better.'

Maggi was still stunned by the fact that her father had called Adam her husband; for so long her parents hadn't talked about him at all, and even recently, when he had begun to encroach on their lives again, he had only ever been referred to as Adam, or 'that man'. Her husband... He wasn't her husband!

'Adam's right, Daddy.' It almost choked her to say it! 'Mamá will come back and sit with you.' She squeezed his hand, thinking how defenceless he looked lying there so weakly in the bed.

He looked as if he was about to continue arguing, and then he gave a weary sigh of capitulation as they looked at him so determinedly. 'You'll come back, Adam?' he prompted.

'I told you I would.' He nodded abruptly. 'You just concentrate on getting better. The rest of us can look after ourselves,' he added pointedly. 'I'll make sure they're both okay, Ted,' he reassured the older man firmly.

'Thanks,' Maggi's father accepted gratefully. 'You always could be relied on in a crisis! With two headstrong females alone in the house, anything could happen!' Once again he attempted to joke.

Maggi still felt dazed when she found herself outside in the waiting-room, only vaguely aware of her mother—who was much calmer—and Mark, as they sat there quietly talking together.

'I think Ted would like you to go back and sit with him, Maria,' Adam informed her gently. 'He's fine,' he offered at her panicked expression, 'but I don't think too many people around him just now is such a good idea.'

'The doctor has been in and told us the same thing.' Mark was the one to answer him. 'Perhaps it would be better, in those circumstances, instead of both of you getting exhausted—' he spoke to the two women '—if you took it in turns to sit with him?'

'Good idea, Mark,' Adam agreed briskly. 'I suggest you stay here with Maria so that you can drive her home later—'

'I'm not leaving Ted,' Maggi's mother cut in adamantly.

'No one is suggesting that you should,' Adam replied kindly. 'But if you sit with Ted now, while he's awake, Magdalena can take over from you later. I'll take Magdalena home now, for a few hours' rest, and then we can come back later when you need a break.'

Her mother's mouth set stubbornly. 'I—'

'Don't you think that would be the best plan, Magdalena?' Adam prompted her pointedly as he accurately predicted her mother's objections to his suggestion.

She had to admit she wasn't too keen on 'I'll take Magdalena home now', or 'then we can come back later when you need a break', but she couldn't argue with the sense of her mother and herself taking turns to sit with her father. Otherwise she would end up with both her parents in hospital—her father recovering from a heart attack, her mother suffering from exhaustion!

She moved to her mother's side, putting a comforting arm about her shoulders. 'Adam's right, Mamá. You aren't going to do Daddy any good if you make yourself ill.' She glanced at her wristwatch. 'It's four o'clock now; I can come back at nine.'

'Make it midnight, Magdalena, and then we can sit with your father through the night while your mother gets some sleep.' Adam looked at her challengingly as she bit back her reaction to his intervention.

His suggestion—if it had been a suggestion!—about returning at midnight was a practical one. Having him accompany her back to the hospital at midnight was not! But she wasn't about to dispute the point in front of her already distraught mother...

'I think that's probably best, Mamá,' she told her mother gently. 'Or I could stay with you now, if you would prefer it,' she offered as her mother still looked confused. 'And—'

'No! No.' Her mother shook her head. 'Adam is right. You go. Mark can stay here with me. Come back at midnight,' she added distractedly, before going back into Maggi's father's room, all of them outside—and their conversation probably forgotten the moment she did so.

'Maggi—'

'Stay with Maria, Mark,' Adam instructed him harshly, tightly gripping Maggi's arm.

Mark shot Adam an impatient look before turning back to Maggi. 'Maggi?' he prompted huskily.

She was finding it difficult to think straight; her whole world seemed to have turned upside down in the last few hours. Her parents had always been there, always indestructible, never—

'I'm taking her home, Mark,' Adam told him determinedly. 'Can't you see she's in shock?'

In shock? Was she? She couldn't think straight, she knew that, was letting Adam make all the decisions. Which wasn't like her at all! But her father had suffered a heart attack today—none of them really needed the results of the tests to know that—and she felt as if her world was falling apart.

'Okay, Adam,' Mark accepted quietly, having studied Maggi's ashen face for several seconds. He moved to her side to put his arms about her and give her a hug. 'It will be fine, Maggi, you'll see,' he assured her. 'It doesn't look as if it was too serious an attack. Keep your chin up.' He smiled with gentle encouragement.

She nodded, distracted. 'It's very good of you to help like this, Mark,' she said gratefully.

'I'm happy to do it. I'm almost one of the family anyway,' he added.

That was true. Over the last three years Mark had become the son her mother and father had never had, and Maggi knew her mother was in safe hands with Mark at her side. 'So you are.' She returned his hug.

'Very touching,' Adam rasped as he strode forcefully at her side down the hospital corridor to the car park.

Maggi spared him only a cursory glance. Such was the depth of her worry and concern over her father that she couldn't even be bothered to ask Adam to remove that proprietorial hold he had on her arm. It wasn't important. None of it was important any more.

Her father could have died today. If Adam hadn't been there, hadn't acted so promptly—

'Don't dwell on the "what ifs", Magdalena,' he advised as he helped her up into the Range Rover. 'Believe me, it does no good whatsoever—except possibly cause you unnecessary heartache!'

Maggi watched him as he closed the car door, grim-faced as he walked around the front of the vehicle to get in behind the steering wheel. She had had so many 'what ifs' where this man was concerned: what if they hadn't crashed that night? What if she hadn't lost their baby? What if she hadn't been told there would probably be no more children? What if she hadn't been confined to a wheelchair? What if there had never been Sue Castle? What if Adam had really loved her…?

Tears blinded her, so that she could no longer focus on Adam's face as he turned her towards him. She could feel the heat of those tears on her cheeks as a sob caught in her throat.

'Oh, hell!' she heard Adam mutter savagely, moments before he gathered her up in his arms and crushed her against his chest. 'It will be all right, Magdalena.' He smoothed her hair down the length of her spine. 'It will be all right! Please don't cry any more; I can't bear it when you cry!' he groaned.

But it seemed that once the tears had started they wouldn't stop, sobs racking her body as she cried and cried. And not just for her father. For all those 'what ifs' too! She had thought she had no more tears left to cry where this man was concerned, had been sure she was all cried out.

But she cried for everything—the past, the present

and the future. A future without the man she had once loved so completely. Because that man hadn't really existed. And he never would…

The tears stopped as abruptly as they had started and she pulled determinedly away from Adam's arms, unable to even look at him, huddling down into her seat now, a tight ball of stubbornly controlled emotion.

She could feel Adam looking at her for several long seconds, could sense his frustration with her, knew how he must hate her withdrawal from him, his inability to be in control of this situation. But she steadfastly refused to look at him, staring sightlessly out of the side window, lost in her own misery, uncaring of how Adam felt or what he wanted from her.

She felt numb, barely aware of the passing countryside as they drove back to her parents' home, not seeing the houses as they entered Lowell, a town probably as yet unaware that one of the doctors in their local practice was at this moment a hospital patient himself. Maggi still found it difficult to accept herself. Parents were invincible, immortal—at least, she had thought hers were.

She shouldn't have left the hospital, should have stayed with her father. Anything might happen to him while she was away.

'Nothing is going to happen, Magdalena.' Adam spoke firmly—making Maggi realise that she must have spoken her panic out loud. 'Your father's condition is stable. Your mother is with him. You'll be better able to cope with sitting with him through the night once you're refreshed from sleep.'

Sleep? She would never be able to sleep. She had

only agreed to this arrangement in the first place so as not to put any more strain on her mother.

She didn't want anything to eat or drink either, when Adam offered to get her something once they were inside the house. She just wanted to be alone.

'I don't think so,' Adam told her grimly.

She had spoken her thoughts out loud once again! She didn't even know what she was doing any more. Even more reason for her to be alone...

'I'm not going anywhere, Magdalena.' Adam spoke harshly. 'So get used to the idea.'

'I—'

'I promised your father I would go back with you later,' he reminded her abruptly. 'I don't intend letting him down.'

Adam had become morally correct! It would be funny—if she could find anything funny at the moment. But she couldn't. And she was too emotionally weary to argue with him any more.

'Do what you please, Adam,' she told him tiredly. 'You usually do anyway!' She turned away, moving up the stairs like an automaton, just wanting the privacy of her bedroom.

'You'll be more comfortable if you get undressed and into bed properly,' Adam told her as she lay on top of the bed fully dressed—the first indication she had that he had followed her up the stairs to her bedroom.

She gave him a startled look. Her bedroom, the bedroom she had occupied since she was a small child—except during her brief marriage to Adam— looked so small with his all-pervasive presence. She half rose off the bed.

'Stay where you are.' He halted her movements, crossing the room to her side. 'Magdalena—'

'Go away, Adam!' She turned away from him, her face half buried in the pillow, her voice thick again with unshed tears, her throat aching with the effort it took not to break down completely. She mustn't cry. She mustn't! Because this time she might not be able to stop...

The mattress sank a little as Adam sat beside her on the bed and took her into his arms again, holding her softness against his chest. 'I'm not going anywhere, Magdalena,' he reminded her against her hair. 'I went once, against my better judgement; I'll not be sent away again. By anyone!' His arms tightened about her. 'Get used to the idea, Magdalena; I'm staying right here!'

She didn't know what he was talking about, didn't care what he was saying. His warmth engulfed her as he lay full-length beside her on the bed. She lay stiff and unyielding in his arms, her eyes tightly closed, terrified, stricken by her unmistakable reaction to his closeness.

'Relax, Magdalena,' he instructed her. 'Just what sort of man do you think I am? What sort of monster have I become in your mind?' he added. 'I'm only going to hold you, nothing else. Do you understand?'

Her eyes remained tightly closed, her body rigid and cold. Because there had been one 'what if' she hadn't included in her thoughts earlier—because she hadn't dared! What if she should find she still wanted Adam as desperately as she could feel that she did at this moment...?

CHAPTER NINE

IT WAS dark when Maggi woke up. The bedside clock showed it was after midnight, and it took her several disorientated seconds to realise that the heavy weight across her breasts was in fact an arm. Adam's arm. One of his legs was also draped across both of her legs.

Almost as if, even in sleep, he was ensuring that she wouldn't escape him…!

Quite when—or how—she had fallen asleep in his arms she didn't know; she had been utterly convinced she would never be able to do so in such close proximity to him. But somehow emotional exhaustion had been stronger than her desire to be free of Adam, and she had slept.

Emotional exhaustion…! Her father—

'I telephoned the hospital a short time ago.' Adam spoke softly in the darkness. 'Your father's condition is still stable and your mother is asleep. They advised that you delay going back in until later this morning.'

How had he known she was awake, let alone what she was thinking? As far as she was aware, she hadn't so much as moved a muscle. How had Adam ever known? He just had…

'I'm going back now.'

'I told them that,' Adam assured her dryly. 'We'll leave shortly.'

'I told you—'

'Stop arguing, woman,' he cut in wearily. 'You never used to be so damned cantankerous! Believe it or not, I've always been very fond of your father; I have great respect for him. And that being the case, I intend going back to the hospital anyway. With you or without you,' he added as she would have spoken again.

Once again she hadn't the strength to argue. Adam could do what he liked—he usually did anyway!— and so would she. Except that his arm still lay across her breasts, his leg over both of hers... In fact, he was too damned close altogether!

He moved in the semi-darkness; a light was on in the hallway outside her slightly open bedroom door, showing him leaning up on one elbow as he looked down at her. Closer still!

'You're so beautiful, Magdalena,' he told her, his hand moving to caress the silky darkness of her hair.

His voice was seductive in its softness, and Maggi felt that familiar fluidity in her body, that melting sensation in every bone. Her mouth tightened as she looked up at him. 'I am now—'

'You were always beautiful, damn it!' he rasped harshly, his hand tightening briefly in her hair. 'The way I thought about you, felt about you, that never changed, Magdalena. You're the one who changed!'

'I didn't have any choice about it.'

'Yes, you did, damn you.' He was angry now. 'You could have stayed my little blackbird, continued to fly—'

'I couldn't even walk, let alone fly!' she returned as furiously, stung by his use of that name. 'Blackbird' was an endearment only used between them during their most intimate moments.

He rose up darkly in front of her. 'I think your father was wrong three years ago,' he ground out savagely, both hands grasping her shoulders now. 'I should have stayed around, shaken you out of this self-pity that seems to have become such a part of you.'

'How dare you?' Her eyes flashed deeply blue. 'You have no idea—'

'I have every idea of what you've physically gone through,' he interrupted. 'Made it my business to know. But no one mentioned this monumental self-pity, this— I don't think so, Magdalena.' He moved easily—and swiftly!—to fend off the swinging arc of her hand as she tried to slap him. 'I really don't think so,' he murmured, before his head lowered and his mouth claimed possession of hers.

Fire. Melting hot fire. Her body, every single particle of her being, was burning. For Adam. For the shattering of the senses she knew she could find only in his arms. That she *was* finding!

Her body reacted to Adam's caresses as if it were only yesterday that they had made love, like a perfect ballet, their bodies moving to meld together. Adam's mouth plundered hers as his hand moved to cup her breast, his thumb easily finding the throbbing tip, and heat such as Maggi had never known before coursed through her body.

She felt out of control, more so even than that first time with Adam all those years ago—her first time with a man. He had been so gentle with her that night, so careful of her innocence, bringing her again and again to the point of ecstasy before slowly soothing their passion to a slow fire, making sure he didn't hurt her when his full possession finally came.

He was like that with her again now, his hands gentle but assured as he slowly but surely removed each piece of her clothing before removing his own. He was beautiful in the half-light, all golden muscle and sinew, his eyes dark as he looked down at her nakedness.

Was she different to him now? she wondered self-consciously. The accident had left scars, a mesh of silver lines that spread over her stomach and thighs, scars she had become accustomed to but which Adam had never seen before. Would he find her ugly now? Would he think—?

She gave an audible gasp as Adam slowly lowered his head and began to kiss that network of scars, each and every one of them. Her body instinctively arched towards his mouth, asking for more.

'Adam…!' She groaned her desperation, her body hot and wet, wanting Adam inside her, needing— Oh, how she needed!

His hands moved up to caress her breasts, his mouth still moist and warm on her skin, his tongue tracing the line of every single one of those silvery scars, until finally—finally he was kissing her as she wanted to be kissed. The whole world seemed to tilt wildly out of control as pleasure coursed through every part of her, emanating from the fire at her thighs out to her fingertips and the very tips of her toes.

If she had died and gone to heaven then she wanted to stay there, never wanted to be anywhere else but here in Adam's arms, communicating with him in a way that had always been right between them. Once they had never been too tired, or too at odds with each other, to make love in this magical, mind-blowing way. Never——

She gasped again as Adam easily moved inside her, filling her totally, totally possessing her.

'Look at me, Magdalena.' He spoke hoarsely above her, and she realised for the first time that her eyes were tightly closed.

He was magnificent above her—dark hair tousled over his forehead, his eyes deep, fathomless pools, a slight flush to the harsh lines of his cheeks, his lips full, the dark column of his throat taut, his shoulders wide and muscular, hair curling damply across his chest.

'I want you to know it's me making love to you, Magdalena,' he told her harshly. 'And not some pale substitute.'

What——?

'It's me, Magdalena—Adam,' he muttered gruffly as his mouth plundered the softly scented warmth of her throat. 'I could always reach you this way, couldn't I?' he murmured with satisfaction, even as his body began to move in hers with slow, pleasure-giving strokes, making further thought on Maggi's part impossible.

They fitted so well together, Adam's hardness a perfect match for her warm softness, those slow movements driving her insane as she felt the pleasure building, rising, threatening to burst out of control.

'Adam, I can't—I—Adam...!' She clung desperately to his shoulders as every part of her exploded, the pleasure, the aching, burning pleasure, almost too much to bear.

'Yes, Magdalena,' Adam groaned encouragingly. 'Give to me, my darling. Fly, blackbird. Fly!'

She didn't have any choice, possessed in every way possible as Adam's mouth came down on hers, his tongue in harmony with the movements of his body.

She had thought her pleasure over, but it wasn't so. Adam brought her to that peak twice more before his own body shuddered beyond his control, hard inside her now, moving, moving, until— The sensation that engulfed them both was deeper and stronger than anything Maggi had ever known before, and Adam's cry of pleasure was almost one of pain as he joined her on her high plateau, his body shaking as he enjoyed their final moments of ecstasy.

They clung damply together in the aftermath, a tangle of arms and legs, hers so pale and fragile, his so tanned and strong, their breathing deep and ragged in the silence of the night.

Reality came back all too suddenly for Maggi, and she began to cry softly as an ache of another kind took over. This man was the reason why, when Mark had tried to rekindle their relationship two years ago, she hadn't been able to respond, why he had finally fallen in love with Andrea. This man was the reason there could never be anyone else for her. This man was the reason she was destined to spend the rest of her life alone.

Because what had happened between them just now could never be repeated with someone else. Here, naked in each other's arms, they could communicate in a way many people never did, could understand each other perfectly. Apart, fully clothed, they had nothing to say to each other.

'Don't move,' Adam groaned into her neck as she would have done exactly that. 'I like you being part of me. The other half of me!'

But she wasn't, and never would be. Adam was only back in her life now because he wanted her to sing with him.

The tears were no longer silent and a sob choked at her throat, her whole body shaking with grief.

Adam raised his head to look into her face, frowning as he saw the river of tears that wet the paleness of her cheeks. His hand moved up to touch those tears, bringing the wetness of his fingertips to his mouth, tasting the salt there.

His eyes were the colour of slate as his gaze returned to her face. 'I wish I could fool myself into thinking these are tears of happiness, that the intenseness of the pleasure we just shared has made you cry like it used to. But they aren't, are they?' he said evenly, in a statement rather than a question. 'We haven't done anything wrong, Magdalena. I'm still your husband; you're still my wife.'

'And you have Celia. And I have Mark.' Once again she hoped Mark and Andrea would forgive her. She just felt so defenseless, lying here in Adam's arms, their bodies still joined together.

Adam's eyes glittered in the semi-darkness. 'Mark's been spreading his poison, has he?' he grated.

'Mark…?' She frowned. 'Oh, you mean because of Celia Mayes.' Her brow cleared. 'Mark hasn't said anything to me about her.' And, to give her friend his due, he hadn't, even though he had obviously known about the other woman's role in Adam's life all along.

Mark would never deliberately hurt her. Whereas this man...

Or perhaps it hadn't been deliberate three years ago? Perhaps Adam had hoped she would never know of his betrayal of their marriage with Sue Castle? He had underestimated the other woman's determination where he was concerned.

Maggi had never fooled herself that the female singer had told her of her affair with Adam because she felt remorse over what had happened between them; Sue had obviously decided she liked her career linked to Adam's, and any return by Maggi would have put an end to that. Oh, no, Maggi had never been naïve enough to underestimate Sue's motives in telling of her relationship with Adam. But that didn't change the fact that Adam had betrayed her and their marriage vows.

Adam held her shoulders. 'Then who else has been spreading such malicious rumours?' he demanded.

'No one,' she answered him impatiently. 'I overheard you and Mark talking at Celia's house that day.' It was very difficult to have this sort of conversation when their bodies were still joined in this intimate way! Although Adam didn't seem to be having the problem with it that she was...!

'Eavesdroppers never hear any good of themselves—or other people!' he bit out disgustedly. 'And I learnt long ago not to believe everything I hear. I'm close to both Celia and Geoffrey, and godfather to their two sons. I absolutely adore those two little—'

'I don't want to know!' Somehow she found the strength to push him away from her, feeling a moment of grief as his body left hers. 'Your life, and who you have in it, is none of my business,' she told him with cold dismissal as she rolled over to her side of the bed and sat up, conscious now of those silvery scars Adam had kissed during their lovemaking, quickly standing up to gather up her robe from where it lay across the bedroom chair, pulling it on and tightly fastening the belt before facing him again.

Her breath caught in her throat as she did so; he was so beautiful. So golden and tautly muscled, not an ounce of fat on his powerfully built body.

She closed her eyes—and her heart!—to the effects of that body. 'I have to get back to the hospital.'

'What happened just now?' he demanded harshly.

She didn't want to think about what had happened just now! Perhaps later, when she could be alone with the painful memories, but not at this moment, not in front of Adam.

She shrugged dismissively. 'A natural response when one has brushed closely with death—'

'I don't accept that!' he told her savagely as he stood up. 'This had nothing to do with death—and everything to do with life. You—'

'Exactly,' she agreed abruptly. 'We human beings have always used sex as a statement of our own immortality.'

'Except that wasn't sex, Magdalena,' he said softly. 'We made love. Beautifully orchestrated, unadulterated love.'

She stiffened at that last phrase; adultery was what Adam was good at. 'You're living in fantasy land, Adam, if you choose to believe that,' she scorned to hide her pain. 'It was good, well-practised sex! And if Mark had been the one to drive me back from the hospital earlier the two of us wouldn't even be having this conversation!'

Adam was suddenly very still, dangerously so. 'Are you saying that if Mark had driven you back here he would have been the one sharing your bed?'

'Of course I'm saying that!' she dismissed easily. 'Now, if you'll excuse me, I have to shower before going back to the hospital.' She turned her back on him and walked away.

As she took each step towards the bathroom she expected to be wrenched round by Adam and made to listen as he forced her to admit that their love-making hadn't been the basic need she was insisting it was.

But she reached the bathroom without that happening, hardly able to believe her luck, glancing back at Adam once she reached the safety of the bathroom doorway. He wasn't looking at her; in fact he was sitting on the side of the bed with his back towards her. Slumped would be a better way of describing him, his shoulders hunched over, his head bent.

She felt a moment's remorse for the harsh things she had just said about their lovemaking. Then she determinedly dismissed that remorse; to admit, even accept, that they had made love would be to utterly destroy all the defences she had managed to build against him over the last three years. She needed those. Couldn't survive on her own, without them.

She closed the door firmly behind her, pushing the bolt of the lock firmly into place. Not that she thought Adam would invade her privacy, not now. But she needed that barrier between them—needed the lock put back on her heart.

She ran the shower, standing beneath its cleansing cascade, washing the feel and taste of Adam from her body, refusing to cry the tears that would have mingled with that hot spray. She couldn't cry now, wouldn't be able to stop once she started.

Adam was fully dressed and sitting at the kitchen table drinking coffee when she came downstairs twenty minutes later. He didn't even glance at her as she strode into the room wearing fitted black denims and a cropped black jumper, standing up to woodenly pour her a cup of coffee from the freshly brewed pot that stood on the percolator.

Maggi didn't care to ask how he had located the coffee or the cups. In fact, she didn't care to talk at all. The expression on Adam's face was one of complete unapproachability.

She sat down to drink the coffee, neither of them speaking. Because there were no words...

'Perhaps you should go back to the hospital; I'll drive you as soon as you're ready.' Adam was the one to finally break the silence, his voice cold and remote.

He wasn't looking at her but at something on the kitchen wall over her left shoulder. A brief glance at that spot showed a line of tiles, one no different from another... Adam couldn't even look at her!

'Perhaps I should drive myself—'

'Perhaps you should!' He jumped in on her hesitant suggestion. 'My being there will serve no purpose—except maybe to annoy you!' he acknowledged hardly.

He was so distant, so totally removed from the man who had made love with her such a short time ago.

That was what she had wanted, wasn't it? She had wanted him distanced, wanted him far away! Except— 'I thought my father wanted to speak to you?' She frowned.

Something flashed briefly in the dark grey of his eyes. Anger? Pain? Dismissal? She couldn't tell. Whatever it was, the emotion was quickly masked, that unreadable expression firmly back in its place.

'It was nothing important,' he said coolly. 'Perhaps you could tell your father that for me—that it's not important. Exactly that,' he added, as if coming to some sort of decision. 'He'll understand, I'm sure.'

Which was more than Maggi did. But Adam wasn't about to explain anything, least of all to her. In fact, he looked as if talking to her at all was an effort! The sooner they went their separate ways the better!

But even so... 'Daddy was so specific—'

'Just give him the message, damn it!' Adam stood up abruptly. 'I told you, he'll understand.' He began to prowl up and down the kitchen.

And 'prowl' was the only way to accurately describe his brooding movements. Like a caged animal.

He was not in the best of moods for Maggi to get a sensible answer out of him, she readily admitted. But now that some of the shock of yesterday had worn off—and she desperately wanted to avoid even thinking about the two of them in bed together a short time ago!—she knew that Adam, and probably Adam alone, had the answers to her questions.

'I don't understand why Daddy went to see you yesterday.' She gave a slow shake of her head.

'There's nothing to understand,' Adam grated. 'He was as upset as you obviously were about the newspapers. I think he imagined I had set you up too. Maybe he wanted me out of your life. I really don't know, Magdalena; he collapsed before he got around to telling me why he was there.'

'I see,' Maggi said slowly, not altogether sure he was telling her the whole truth. Although it made sense; her father had obviously been upset yesterday morning about the newspapers, and he was protective enough of her to do something like that. Although there was still the puzzle of how her father had known where to find Adam...

Adam shook his head, his expression grim. 'I doubt that you do. I doubt that you believe me about those photographs in the papers, either. I'm getting used to the fact that you don't believe a word I say. Nevertheless, I'll repeat what I said earlier—I did not have anything to do with the photographer being there the day before yesterday. I've been just as inundated with reporters as you have.' He grimaced with feeling. 'But you don't have to believe that, either.'

'I believe you.' She was taken aback at his vehemence; he was seriously angry. He had been since she'd made that provocative statement concerning Mark. But what else was she supposed to do? Admit she hadn't so much as been out with another man during the last three years, let alone wanted to go to bed with one? She couldn't have left herself that vulnerable!

Even if it *was* true...

It was also true that as soon as Adam had lain down beside her on the bed earlier tonight she had known she wanted him. Just as if none of the past had ever happened. As if all of those 'what ifs' had come true...

His mouth twisted. 'I'm sure that's supposed to give me some satisfaction—but it doesn't!' His eyes glittered flintily. 'You'll get your recording contract— your solo recording contract,' he added pointedly. 'If both of us refuse to work together they'll offer you the solo contract that you want.'

Maggi frowned. 'And is that what you're saying you'll do now?'

His jaw clenched. 'Do you want me to put it down in black and white and sign the damned thing?' he rasped savagely.

'Of course not.' She grimaced at his barely leashed anger.

'Then what the hell do you want, Magdalena?' he prompted. 'Or is it that you still don't believe me? Do you think I'll go back on what I've just said—is that it?'

His capitulation seemed too good to be true; she admitted that. She had never known Adam to back off from a fight, and he had seemed so determined...

'I can see that you do!' he exploded, tired of waiting for her reply. 'Fine,' he snapped tautly, looking about the kitchen with narrowed eyes before spotting the notepad her mother always kept next to the refrigerator so that she could write down things to buy when she went shopping as she realised she needed them.

Adam picked up the notepad and pen, scribbling down a few impatient words before scrawling his signature along the bottom. 'It may not be a legal document—' he thrust the notepad at her '—but I'll stand by my written word.'

Maggi held the pad with trembling fingers, almost afraid to look down and see what he had written.

Adam gave a scornful snort. 'It says I'm out of your life, Magdalena, both professionally and personally. And once I've walked out that door it will be true. But until I have...' He strode across the short distance that separated them, dragging her roughly into his arms. 'You're such a fool, Magdalena,' he told her. 'Such a cowardly fool!'

She opened her mouth to protest at being called a coward, only to find Adam's mouth possessing hers, his kiss hard, nothing at all like their lovemaking had been such a short time ago.

As he continued to kiss her in that way she knew the difference between tender lovemaking and a need to punish. Adam had made love to her earlier! It hadn't been sex, as she had told him it was, but love.

Did that mean that Adam loved her...?

CHAPTER TEN

MAGGI was dazed, totally dazed, when at last Adam lifted his head, and she stared up at him wordlessly.

'Don't look so shocked, Magdalena,' he derided. 'And cheer up.' His knuckles touched her lightly under the chin and then he released her. 'You've got what you wanted. What you always wanted,' he added bitterly. 'I'm out of here. Out of your life. Out of your career. Out of our marriage.' He ran a weary hand through the dark thickness of his hair. 'I'll sign your divorce papers, Magdalena. Free both of us.'

She didn't understand. Something was wrong here. Oh, so very wrong!

'Just don't send me an invitation to your wedding when the time comes; I may be family, but in the circumstances it would be in pretty poor taste. I'll send the two of you one of the many sets of salad servers you'll receive and never use. But don't ask me to dance—or sing!—at your wedding.'

He was talking about when she married Mark. He was Mark's cousin, and therefore family. But there would never be a wedding to Mark. Not with her as the bride anyway.

Adam was leaving her life. It was what she wanted, as he'd said it was... The torment of having him back in her life was over.

Then why wasn't she jumping for joy? Because she

142

should be, should be glad her life would be free of him once and for all. Hell had frozen over!

He gave a laugh edged with bitterness at her continued silence. 'I had better be on my way. Having rendered you speechless, it seems as good a time as any to go.' He turned to leave.

As jokes went, it was pretty feeble. It made Maggi feel like crying instead of laughing. And, amazingly, so did his leaving.

'What did you say?' He turned at the doorway.

Once again she had spoken out loud without realising it. Although barely audibly, it seemed.

What had she mumbled...? 'I'm not marrying Mark,' she said more clearly, the words sounding as if they came through sandpaper.

'Aren't you? Oh, well, I can't say I exactly blame you.' He gave an understanding nod. 'Marriages aren't so easy to get out of, are they? Even nowadays. Your parents seem pretty resigned to your relationship on its present basis, so why bother to change it?'

'You don't understand.' But neither did she, not exactly. What would she achieve by telling Adam that Mark had only ever been a friend to her, that he was marrying her physiotherapist? Because her thoughts earlier had been a mere madness of the moment; of course Adam didn't love her. If he loved her, he wouldn't be agreeing to the divorce.

He gave a grimace. 'I don't think I want to, Magdalena. Not any more. For a while I thought— Stupid.' He shook his head. 'Be happy, love. Enjoy your life. You deserve it.'

And he was gone. Just like that. And the vacuum

he left behind him was one that Maggi knew would never be filled. Never in her lifetime...

Her parents were both still asleep when she got back to the hospital, and the nurse assured her all was well before Maggi went in search of Mark in the waiting-room.

His gaze instinctively moved past and behind her as she quietly entered the room.

'Adam isn't here.' She flatly answered the question he hadn't yet asked.

Dark brows rose. 'Is he having trouble parking the car?'

'I drove myself.' She sat down heavily, still not absolutely sure how she had got here. She didn't remember the drive at all, supposed she must have come in her BMW. But she didn't remember parking it outside the hospital either...

Mark looked at her closely, missing nothing of the shadows beneath her eyes, the paleness of her cheeks, the slight tremble to her hands as she pushed the dark thickness of her hair back over her shoulders.

He placed one of his hands over both of hers as they lay limply in her lap. 'What happened, Maggi?' he prompted softly.

She squeezed her eyes tightly shut, willing the tears not to fall, but her lashes were nonetheless spiked with the wetness of them as she looked up at Mark.

'Oh, Maggi, love,' he groaned, before gently enfolding her in his arms, letting her cry as the sobs racked her body. 'The bastard,' he muttered as the tears continued to flow. 'The lousy, rotten—'

'You don't understand, Mark. Adam and I— We— I—'

'I understand completely, Maggi,' he cut in angrily. 'My dear cousin acted in his usual selfish way and took advantage of the situation. Nothing more and nothing less!'

'He's gone, Mark.' She raised her head to look at him. 'Gone for good,' she added shakily. 'He's agreed to the divorce, the solo recording career. Everything.'

'Then I don't— Maggi?' Mark grasped her arms as his eyes remorselessly searched the anguish of her expression. 'You still love him,' he muttered incredulously.

He had a right to be incredulous. She was herself. However, she knew it to be the truth. She loved Adam. Would always love him. But he was finally, and irrevocably, gone from her life.

She should be feeling ecstatic at that knowledge— and instead she was devastated.

'Maggi, sometimes the mind plays tricks on us,' Mark reasoned gently. 'You and Adam always were physically—volatile together. Don't be deceived into thinking what happened between the two of you last night was anything other than that.'

She wasn't deceived, not by anything she had felt yesterday evening. Or by how she still felt. 'Don't worry, Mark.' She gave him a watery smile. 'I'm not going to fall apart or anything remotely like that.' She gave a shaky laugh when he didn't look convinced. 'Have you ever known me to fall apart, Mark?' she chided teasingly.

He grimaced. 'It was a very close thing last time.'

'And look how far I've come since then,' she dismissed firmly. 'My career can finally move forward, Mark,' she said encouragingly. 'It's what we've both worked so hard for.'

He nodded. 'I just wish you looked happier about it.'

'Once my father is on his feet again and back home, then I'll look happier. You'll see,' she added with certainty.

She knew from experience that the only way to deal with the part of her heart that belonged to Adam was to firmly close the door on it. It might not be the healthiest thing to do, but it was the route that caused her the least pain.

Unfortunately, the first thing her father did, when he woke from his healing sleep, was to ask for Adam!

Maggi and Mark had kept a silent vigil for the rest of the night as her parents slept. Her mother had been the first to wake, just after six o'clock, and Maggi had persuaded her to go off with Mark to the hospital canteen to get some breakfast; the last thing she wanted herself was food. She had a sick feeling in the pit of her stomach that refused to go away.

Consequently she was with just the attendant nurse when her father woke up a short time later. His colour was much better, that grey having faded from his cheeks, although he still looked small and defenceless against the white of the hospital sheets.

'Cheer up,' he told her lightly, alerting her to his wakefulness. 'It may never happen!'

It already had—she had fallen in love with her own husband all over again! Adam had told her to cheer up, too. No! She couldn't think about Adam. It would only cause her more pain.

'Where's Adam?' her father asked astutely as he realised she was alone.

She swallowed hard. 'He—he had to be somewhere else,' she replied awkwardly.

Her father frowned. 'But he promised he would come back.'

'Daddy, promise or no promise, he has no place in our lives!' She stood up agitatedly. 'He hasn't for a long time.'

'But—'

'Daddy, Adam and I have talked,' she said evenly. 'And we both think it best if Adam gets on with his life and leaves all of us to get on with ours. He's agreed to the divorce, Daddy,' she added conclusively.

He slumped back against the pillows. 'I can't believe that,' he said, obviously puzzled.

'Believe it,' she told him lightly, going back to the side of the bed to take one of his hands into hers. 'It's over, Daddy. Can we just leave it at that?'

He still looked unconvinced. 'Is that the way Adam feels too?'

'I told you, he's agreed to the divorce,' she confirmed.

'But did the two of you talk—really talk? About everything?' His hand tightened on hers.

If the two of them carried on talking about Adam much longer she was going to break down and cry once more.

'The past is—exactly that,' she told her father. 'Three years is just too long, Daddy. There's nothing left.' Except her love for Adam—and the desire he still felt for her. But, as Mark had said, that part of

their relationship had always been volatile; there had
to be more than that. Unfortunately, on Adam's part,
there wasn't.

Her father looked at her searchingly. 'You don't
love him?'

'No stress, no strain, no worries...' Maggi recalled
the doctor's words. If her father knew how she still
felt about Adam he would be sure to worry.

She swallowed hard, her smile forced. 'I don't love
him,' she said tightly. 'Maybe I never did. I was very
young when I met him.'

'But, Maggi—'

'Daddy, I made a mistake five years ago when I
married Adam, but I don't have to go on paying for
it for the rest of my life.' She squeezed his hand encouragingly. 'With the divorce imminent, that chapter
of my life can finally be closed.'

He gave a resigned sigh in the face of her indomi-
table certainty. 'If you're sure that's what you
want...?'

'I'm absolutely sure,' she told him emphatically.

The best thing for her to do, where Adam was concerned, was not to talk about him, and not to think
about him either if she could help it. As she had just
told her father, that chapter of her life was well and
truly closed.

Over the next few weeks it really seemed as if it was.
Her father's health improved by leaps and bounds, so
much so that after a week he was allowed out of hospital. It was a happy day for all of them when he came
home.

The record company contacted her too, and the recording of her solo album was scheduled to begin the following week. Evidence indeed that Adam meant to keep his word. The signed piece of paper he had thrust at her in the kitchen that night was consigned to the back of one of her drawers in her bedroom. One day she might be able to look at it again, although not, she was sure, without vividly recalling all that had taken place before it...

Because Adam had also signed and returned the divorce papers to her lawyer...

It was the only jarring note in a time filled with positives, and in its own way it too was a positive. Although it would be some time before Maggi could look on it as such. Most of her adult life had been spent as Adam's wife, and it would be strange, once their divorce was final, for that no longer to be the case.

The first time she appeared as a guest singer on a television show, and a single red rose didn't appear, she felt a sickening jolt in the pit of her stomach. Adam really had gone from her life.

It was what she had wanted for so long, but now that it had happened she felt strangely bereft.

Then she became caught up in all the hard work of recording her album, moving temporarily into a hotel in London and working so hard that she returned every evening with only enough energy to eat a meal in her room before collapsing into bed. December had seemed a long way off when it was first decided that would be the rush-release date of her album, but it now seemed to be approaching all too rapidly.

Mark, as her manager, had also lined up a number of television appearances in advance of the album's release, giving her added publicity—although any chat shows involved were accepted only with the proviso that her relationship with Adam would not be discussed.

'You're starting to look really tired,' Andrea told her concernedly one evening as she and Mark drove her to a television studio for yet another of those interviews. 'I've told Mark he's pushing you too hard.' She frowned at her fiancé. She was a tall, leggy redhead, with a sprinkling of freckles across her nose that added a touch of mischief to her classically beautiful face.

In truth, Maggi was finding it all a bit much, had found it difficult to get out of bed at all this morning! The mornings were dark now, and her bed had been cosy and warm; she had just wanted to curl up and go back to sleep. But she hadn't, had forced herself to get up. Now she only had this couple of hours at the television studio before she could do what she had wanted to do all day—and that was go back to bed!

'It isn't for long.' Maggi smoothly defended Mark, knowing how protective of her patients—even ex-patients—Andrea could be. 'Another couple of weeks and the album will be finished.'

'And then you'll have even more public appearances to do.' Andrea frowned. 'I don't—'

'Will you just concentrate on your approaching wedding, and not worry so much about me?' Maggi put in laughingly, knowing the other couple were busy organising their big day. In fact, they were taking a break from that pressure this evening and treating themselves to an evening out, going on to have a quiet dinner together once they had delivered Maggi to the studio. 'I'm going to get this show over with, take a taxi back to the hotel, have a long soak in the bath and then go to bed. By tomorrow I'll be fine again.' She would make sure she was!

'But—'

'Hey, I'm not your patient any more,' Maggi teased the other woman. 'And if you don't stop fussing I shall refuse to be your bridesmaid!'

'No, you won't,' Andrea said with certainty; the two women were firm friends. 'From the way you are now, you look as if you should be—still my patient, I mean.' She looked concerned. 'You look as if you've lost weight over the last few weeks, and you're still very pale.'

'The weight loss can only be a plus for television; for some reason the camera always makes you look fatter than you really are,' Maggi told her as they came to a halt outside the television studio. 'And make-up will take care of the paleness.'

'An answer for everything!' Mark grinned at her good-naturedly.

'It's a case of having to, with the two of you always fussing over me,' Maggi told them lightly as she got out of the car. 'Enjoy your meal. Forget all about weddings for the evening.'

Mark's eyes went heavenwards. 'The vicar is still in a tizzy because Maggi Fennell is to be one of the bridesmaids. He'll probably make a complete mess of things on the day!'

Maggi was still smiling to herself as she went into the studio building, and perfectly relaxed as she was directed to Make-up. Twenty minutes' rest and relaxation while her make-up was applied, and she would be ready to face the television cameras.

Except that the woman already seated in Make-up made that impossible. Celia Mayes!

Maggi had never met the woman, but she had seen several of her films and would have recognised her anywhere. She was even more beautiful in the flesh, her skin smooth and peachy, her figure voluptuous.

She was also the latest lover in Adam's life...

Maggi felt as if time had suddenly stood still. Celia had to be a guest on the same show as herself...

'Maggi Fennell, isn't it?' the other woman said pleasantly, looking at Maggi with candid blue eyes as she sat down.

Maggi was tongue-tied. Celia Mayes knew who she was! After the publicity concerning Adam and herself several weeks ago, maybe she knew that Maggi had found out about her own friendship with Adam. What did one say to one's ex-husband's mistress...?

She cleared her throat. 'Er—yes,' she confirmed huskily.

Celia Mayes nodded. 'I've always enjoyed your singing.'

Polite conversation—any conversation!—was not something Maggi wished to engage in with Celia, now or at any other time!

'Thank you,' she accepted flatly, wishing herself anywhere but here. She might have dismissed the strain of the last few weeks to Andrea earlier, but she was actually feeling it quite strongly. And this had to be the worst of it!

'I know Adam too, of course,' Celia continued smoothly. 'Thank you, Joanne.' She gave the make-up girl one of her famously heart-stopping smiles as the young woman finished her make-up. 'Very well, in fact,' she added to Maggi, as if the conversation had never been interrupted.

Maggi stiffened. 'So I believe,' she acknowledged abruptly, wishing Celia would just go now that her make-up was complete.

But the actress seemed in no hurry to do that, turning in her seat as Joanne began Maggi's make-up. 'As does my husband, Geoffrey,' she added.

Another cuckolded husband. Perhaps that was an improvement on deceiving your own wife? Although Maggi didn't think so. Adam had no right to intrude on this couple's marriage, especially when there were young children involved. Almost babies, only a year old...

Her gaze hardened as she looked at the other woman. 'I'm aware of that too,' she bit out.

Celia Mayes looked at her consideringly. 'I wonder what else you think you know—?'

'Five minutes, Miss Mayes,' a young boy opened the door to announce importantly, his eyes widening with admiration as he gazed at the actress's exceptional beauty.

'Thank you.' Celia Mayes smiled at him warmly before turning back to Maggi. 'I'm afraid I have to go. But perhaps you would join me for a drink after the show?' she invited smoothly. 'Coffee,' she added encouragingly as Maggi opened her mouth to refuse. 'I rarely drink alcohol since I became a mother,' she added indulgently. 'It wouldn't do to be less than a hundred per cent with my two little bundles of fun!'

Yet she was jeopardising her children's happiness by having an affair with Adam!

She was also, apparently, yet another woman who wanted to boast to Maggi about it. Maggi didn't want to meet her for coffee or anything else; she just didn't want to know.

'Look, I have to go.' Celia Mayes stood up smoothly, beautiful in the black sheath dress she wore. 'But I'll wait for you after the show.' And, with that famous toss of her silky blonde hair, she was gone.

Maggi was still dazed by the whole encounter. She had had no idea who else would be on the show this evening. Although it could have been worse; it could have been Adam himself!

'After the show' came all too quickly for Maggi. She could barely remember doing the television interview, or singing a song at the end, although the interviewer seemed more than pleased as he thanked her afterwards.

Maggi couldn't even recall what she had said, so preoccupied was she with Celia Mayes' motives in wanting to see her after the show. What was it about these women that they felt a need to discuss their relationship with Adam with her? Did it give them some sort of perverse pleasure to tell Maggi of their conquest? Whatever it was, Maggi didn't want to know.

Celia Mayes was waiting downstairs in Reception for her when she came down, flicking idly through a magazine from the table there as she waited. She put it down as soon as she saw Maggi, standing up, a smile curving her lips. 'Ready?'

'Look, Miss Mayes—'

'The name is Celia,' the other woman told her firmly, linking her arm through Maggi's. 'And it's only coffee, Magdalena,' she said as they went outside into the darkened evening.

Maggi moved sharply away from her. 'The name is Maggi,' she snapped, knowing all too well where— and from whom!—the other woman had got her full name. 'And I really don't think—'

'On the contrary—Maggi,' the other woman replied softly. 'I think you think all too much,' she told her enigmatically. 'My car is over here.' She led the way to a pale blue Mercedes. 'Come on, Maggi,' she encouraged as Maggi still held back. 'I don't bite. What have you got to lose?'

Nothing. It was all gone already. Adam. Her marriage. Her one chance of happiness.

She got into the car beside the actress, her mouth set stubbornly as she stared out of the window at the passing traffic.

'I hope you don't mind having coffee at my home.' The actress was the one to finally break the silence. 'Only Geoffrey is away at the moment, and so I've left the boys with a babysitter. Something I don't particularly like doing.'

'I thought you lived in the north of England.' Maggi spoke gruffly; she remembered that house all too well.

The other woman nodded. 'We commute between our house there and the apartment in town. Of course—' she glanced at Maggi '— you've been to the house, haven't you?'

'I visited. Briefly,' Maggi confirmed.

Celia nodded. 'Well, the boys are with me in London at the moment. I don't have a nanny for them. I waited so long for the twins that I have no intention of letting someone else bring them up,' she added determinedly.

This woman was becoming more and more of a puzzle to Maggi. She spoke of her husband and sons with such open affection, and there was such a warmth about her, that Maggi was having trouble disliking her. She wanted to dislike her—certainly didn't want to *like* the woman who was sharing Adam's bed at the moment!

'I'm really not worried about having coffee at all,' she told Celia coldly.

'You're right. We probably deserve something stronger after the nerve-racking experience of being in front of the television cameras!' She grinned as Maggi looked surprised by the description. 'It's something I've never got used to. Geoffrey is always amazed at the fact I can do this at all, because, quite frankly, I don't enjoy it. But the release of a new film needs the help of a little PR.' She shrugged. 'You?'

'Me?' Maggi looked startled at this apparent change of subject.

'Why did you do it?' Celia glanced at her. 'Adam thought it must be to do with your new album.'

She stiffened at the way this woman talked so easily about Adam. It was obvious, from the remark, that if she hadn't known of Celia's appearance in the programme tonight, then Celia had certainly known of hers. It had even been discussed with Adam!

'It is,' she replied distantly.

'Here we are,' Celia said warmly as she drove the

car down into the underground car park. 'I would have liked you to meet the boys, but they're probably fast asleep in bed.'

That suited Maggi perfectly; she had no wish to meet this woman's baby sons. She didn't know what she was doing here at all, felt a little as if she had been run over by a steamroller. She frowned at Celia as they went up in the lift; there was a lot more to her than this charming exterior she chose to present!

'Don't look so worried, Maggi.' Celia smiled as they went into her apartment. 'I just thought we could have a drink and get to know each other a little.'

What on earth was the point of Adam's ex-wife and his current mistress getting to know each other?

'All's quiet,' Celia whispered as she put down her car keys on a small table in the entrance hall. 'A miracle!'

Maggi still had the strangest feeling that under any other circumstances she would have really liked this woman. She was beautiful, charming and good fun. What Maggi had to remember, though, was that Celia was also involved in Adam's life, and that she was a married woman with children.

'Come through,' Celia invited. 'I'll just see you settled before I check on the boys.'

Maggi followed her, still wishing herself far away. She was getting out of here as soon as she was able. One drink and she was going—

'I don't need to introduce you to my babysitter,' Celia told her lightly. 'Everything okay, Adam?'

Adam…?

Adam was this woman's babysitter…?

CHAPTER ELEVEN

MAGGI stared at Adam as he lounged in one of the armchairs in the elegantly furnished room, perfectly relaxed, his legs stretched out in front of him. As if he had done this dozens of times before. Which he probably had! No doubt he spent a lot of his time here when Geoffrey was away.

If she had wanted to leave before, she wanted it even more now. This was becoming an insane situation!

'I brought Maggi back for a drink,' Celia told him conversationally—as if inviting his ex-wife to her home were a perfectly natural thing for her to do. 'Perhaps you could see to that while I check on Michael and Daniel?' she suggested happily, before unhurriedly leaving the room.

Maggi couldn't believe this was happening to her, stared with amazement at Adam as he slowly straightened in the chair, his gaze narrowed on her inscrutably.

He had had his hair cut since the last time she'd seen him, although it was still quite long, with those flecks of grey more visible at his temples. His face looked thinner too, the lines beside his nose and mouth making him look quite grim, and his expression was cold as he continued to survey her.

It was the first time she had seen him since the

evening they'd ended up in bed together, and she, for
one, felt uncomfortable at that memory. Not that
Adam appeared in the least perturbed by the awk-
wardness of the situation...

What was going on here? Had Adam known the
actress would be bringing Maggi back with her? If so,
what was the point? With the divorce imminent, they
had nothing left to say to each other.

Adam stood up slowly, his height, and the power
he exuded, instantly dominating the room. 'What can
I get you?'

She looked at him, her expression one of complete
incomprehension.

'To drink,' he explained slowly.

She didn't want the damned drink. She didn't want
to be here at all!

'Brandy,' he decided, moving the tray of drinks that
stood on the side dresser. 'Here.' He handed her the
bulbous glass. 'The sooner you drink it, the sooner
you can leave,' he added tauntingly as she made no
effort to take the glass from him.

She took the brandy, careful not to touch Adam's
hand, and sipped some of the fiery liquid, instantly
feeling its warmth inside her. Which was just as well;
she had begun to feel as if she was turning into a
block of ice. What on earth had Celia Mayes thought
she was doing by inviting her, knowing full well
Adam was here watching over her sons?

Adam babysitting...! It still seemed incredible to
her. Adam Carmichael acting as babysitter! Although
not just to anyone, to the sons of the woman he was

rumoured to be having an affair with. That wasn't quite the same as just babysitting…

Celia seemed to be taking rather a long time checking on her twins.

'Celia is a romantic,' Adam told Maggi dryly, seeming to guess her panicked thoughts. 'She thinks if she leaves us alone for long enough we'll sort out our differences.' He shook his head, sipping at his own glass of brandy. 'A romantic!' he confirmed disgustedly.

'Especially in the circumstances,' Maggi replied, at last finding her voice again—she felt as if she had been struck dumb for the last half an hour; she had certainly had little to say for herself.

Adam's mouth twisted. 'I'm not about to ask what circumstances you're referring to,' he rasped hardly, 'because I can guess! But if I were you I wouldn't repeat them to Celia, because she's likely to laugh in your face.'

'I don't find any of this funny,' Maggi dismissed impatiently. 'She insisted on being friendly at the television studio—'

'It was a good interview, by the way,' Adam told her lightly. 'And I liked the new song. It should be a good album.'

She didn't want to hear what he thought of her interview earlier tonight, or the song she had sung at the end of it! 'Celia insisted I join her for a drink afterwards. And now, for some reason, she has deliberately left the two of us together.' Maggi was becoming more and more agitated by the situation.

Adam's eyes rested on her red-cheeked face. 'Celia

may have insisted, Magdalena, but you didn't have to give in to it. You have a mind of your own—as I know only too well!—and you could have said no to her invitation.'

'She was very insistent,' Maggi defended irritably.

'And you can be very determined,' he dismissed wryly. 'So what are you doing here?' He quirked mocking brows. 'Don't tell me your curiosity got the better of you?'

Had it? Had some part of her wanted to know, once and for all, exactly what Adam's relationship was with the beautiful actress? A moth drawn to the flame? In this case Adam's mistress...

If so, what sort of masochist was she that she should deliberately put herself through this? Or was it just that the other woman was a link to Adam, no matter how painful? She would have to think through her own actions later, when she was alone; right now she was more concerned with Celia and Adam's motivations!

'I have no curiosity left where you're concerned, Adam,' she told him contemptuously. 'I know all that I need to know!'

'And Celia?' he challenged. 'Do you know all you need to know about her too?'

She felt her cheeks become warm as he hit on exactly why she was here. Against her better judgement, she had found herself actually liking Celia, found a dichotomy in what she had been told about her and the warm friendliness that she actually emanated towards Maggi. Something didn't add up.

'I know nothing about her,' Maggi dismissed determinedly.

'No?' Adam challenged.

'No,' she snapped back, putting down her brandy glass, the alcohol barely touched. 'If I had known you were going to be here this evening I certainly wouldn't have allowed myself to be persuaded into coming!' Her eyes flashed deeply blue. 'We certainly have nothing left to say to each other.'

'Strange, but I always knew you and Celia were going to like each other.' Adam spoke softly. 'And she does like you, Magdalena. Otherwise nothing on this earth would have induced her to invite you to her home.'

'I'm honoured!'

'Sarcasm doesn't become you, Magdalena.'

'*You* don't become me, Adam.' She hurled the words back at him accusingly. 'You bring out the worst in me.'

'And the best, Magdalena,' he said. 'Let's not forget that.'

She hadn't been able to forget that, could still remember all too clearly the magic they had known in each other's arms five weeks ago. Five weeks...? But—

'The very best,' Adam added determinedly, standing all too close now, his hands moving up to grasp her upper arms.

Maggi felt overwhelmed, couldn't breathe, felt as if she was held in a hypnotic spell. This couldn't be happening to her again!

When would it ever end...?

'I'm afraid this young man was playing tricks on you, Adam,' Celia announced as she breezed back into the room, a baby snuggled into her neck. She came to an abrupt halt as she saw the two of them standing so closely together across the room. 'Oops.' She gave an apologetic grimace. 'Shall I go out and come in again?' she suggested teasingly.

Maggi was mortified at being found in such an intimate pose with Adam. Which was ridiculous; if anyone had the right to be found in his arms, it was her. Yet she still felt guilty at being caught out in this way...

Adam moved smoothly away from her, crossing the room to hold out his hands for the baby. 'Daniel Haines, you're going to get me into trouble,' he chided affectionately as the baby turned and moved easily into his arms. 'The deal was that you would be asleep by the time Mummy came home.'

Celia laughed. 'I bet you put the two of them into bed when you heard the car in the driveway!'

Adam grinned at her over the top of the dark head now cuddled into his chest. 'Privileges of the baby-sitter!' he returned unapologetically.

'He's such a softie, Maggi.' The other woman turned and spoke warmly, including her in the conversation. 'But then, you already know that.'

She knew no such thing; she had never found Adam a 'softie', not in their two years of marriage, or in the time since. But perhaps he was different with this woman; he certainly seemed relaxed.

Although it was what she saw now that held her interest at the moment...

The baby in Adam's arms was undoubtedly a beautiful child, with his thick dark hair and eyes just as dark, huge as saucers as he turned to look shyly at the stranger in their midst, a smile suddenly lighting up his face, showing tiny white teeth.

Daniel was absolutely beautiful, and Maggi felt her heart melt at his perfection. And there was another child just like him asleep in the house somewhere! No wonder Celia refused to leave them, or let anyone else help her to bring them up.

Daniel was also, without a doubt, of Oriental parentage. He couldn't possibly—from the photographs Maggi had seen on the mantelpiece of Celia and a rather handsome blond-haired man who had to be Geoffrey Haines—be the couple's natural son...

'Would you like to hold him, Maggi?' Celia invited softly. 'It's all right,' she assured her as Maggi looked alarmed. 'He won't cry. He smiled at you, so he obviously likes the look of you.' She took the baby from Adam and placed him firmly in Maggi's arms. 'Children seem to know instinctively who they can trust. Daniel probably senses you're a part of his uncle Adam.'

Maggi ignored that last remark, totally absorbed with the baby nestled so comfortably against her. He seemed fascinated by her long hair draped silkily over her shoulders, picking up long strands and watching them drop, before grinning at her mischievously. Maggi sat down in an armchair with him, loving the softness of him, the tiny starfish hands that gently touched her skin.

'It suits you, Magdalena.' Adam spoke gruffly.

She looked up at him uncomprehendingly for several seconds, having been totally engrossed in the baby. As his meaning became clear to her all the colour drained from her cheeks. 'You bastard,' she choked disbelievingly. 'How could you?' She stood up abruptly, giving the baby back to his mother. 'Your son is beautiful, Celia. You're a very lucky woman,' she added meaningfully, before turning away and stumbling from the room.

Her arm was grasped and she was spun round to face Adam before she reached the door into the apartment.

'Let go of me, Adam,' she told him between gritted teeth. 'If you have any decency left in you at all, get out of Celia's life. Your relationship with her can only bring her unhappiness.' As it had her. Oh, God, as it had her! She hurt so much at this moment it was almost like a physical pain.

'You don't still believe that rubbish about Celia and me?' Adam cried angrily. 'Have you no sense, woman? Don't you have eyes in your head?' he continued exasperatedly. 'This is a home full of love, Magdalena. It envelops you as soon as you come in the door. There are family photographs everywhere you look. This apartment positively cries out "happy family". I don't believe you can't see and feel that!'

Of course she could see that, and feel it too—that was the reason why she had tried to advise Celia just now to think about what she had. Adam had no right intruding on this happy family.

'I give up on you, Magdalena.' Adam suddenly thrust her away from him. 'Geoffrey is my best friend,

Celia's like a sister to me, I'm godfather to their children, and still you believe I would—' He shook his head disgustedly. 'One day I'm going to find out what I did so wrong that you believe me to be that type of monster!'

'This is all my fault, Adam.' Celia came out into the hallway, the baby asleep in her arms now. 'I thought—' There were tears in those beautiful blue eyes. 'I wanted to make things right for you, Adam,' she told him with soft apology.

'I know you did, love.' He squeezed her arm reassuringly. 'I'm not angry with you.'

No, it was Maggi he was angry with. And he had no right to be. No right at all.

'This is real life, Celia, not one of your films,' Adam added affectionately. 'Reality rarely has a happy ending. You and Geoffrey have one, but mine escaped me,' he said hardly, before turning back to Maggi. 'Don't worry, I meant what I said last time about being out of your life; this won't happen again,' he told her harshly. 'Have a good life, Maggi.' And, with a smoothness that took her totally by surprise, he was the one to very quietly leave.

And Maggi very quietly cried, the tears like hot rivers down her cheeks, blinding her as Celia took her into her arms next to the baby. Both women were crying now, the baby sleeping on unconcernedly between them.

Celia was finally the one to straighten. 'I'll just go and put Daniel down in his cot, and then I'll be back. Go back into the sitting-room, Maggi, and finish your brandy. Then we'll talk.'

Maggi was too distraught to even locate the brandy glass, just sitting down heavily in one of the armchairs.

Adam had called her Maggi. For the first time ever, he had called her Maggi. From their very first meeting he had told her she was too special a lady not to be called by her proper name, that her beauty demanded she be called Magdalena.

She was no longer special to Adam…

She had known it for such a long time, of course, but the stark reality of it—!

'I know why I was crying,' Celia said as she came back into the room. 'But why were you?'

It was too complicated to explain. It was also something Maggi had no intention of explaining to the other woman. 'Adam has that effect on me,' she dismissed self-deprecatingly, in control of her emotions again now.

Celia shook her head. 'I don't understand you two at all. Adam loves you very much. And, after seeing the two of you here, I believe you love him too. So why aren't you together?'

Maggi was taken aback at the directness of the question. But Celia was wrong; Adam didn't love her. Although she accepted that she had been wrong about his relationship with Celia; she'd only had to see the two of them together earlier in the hallway to realise that. There was affection and caring between them, genuine, deep affection, but it was that of brother and sister. She had clearly seen that. No matter what she might have said to Adam to the contrary…

Besides, she had something much more pressing on

her mind at the moment—needed to get home, needed
to talk to her father.

'Celia, I have to go.' She stood up swiftly. 'It was
lovely meeting you, and one of your sons, but I—'

'I wouldn't have those sons if it weren't for Adam,'
Celia interrupted with quiet determination.

Maggi gave her a startled look; exactly what did
she mean by that?

'When Geoffrey and I discovered I couldn't have
children, I was devastated.' Celia held Maggi's gaze
as she spoke. 'I refused to even contemplate the idea
of adoption, dragged Geoffrey to every specialist
there was going in the hope that one of them would
be able to help us. It became an obsession with me.
Every time Geoffrey so much as mentioned adoption,
I distanced myself from him. I wanted our own child,
wanted to feel it grow inside me, to give birth natu-
rally, to hold our child in my arms. In the end,
Geoffrey and I were so far apart we were in danger
of losing our marriage. Sound familiar?' she prompted
gently.

Maggi frowned. Did it? She and Adam had never
got to the stage of going to any specialist; they had
lost probably the only child they would ever have, and
after that she had refused to talk about any of it. Her
pain had been too deep.

'It wasn't the same,' she claimed huskily.

'Oh, Maggi, it *was* the same,' Celia groaned sympathetically. 'Worse, probably. You conceived a child
and then lost it. Don't be angry with Adam for telling
us, Maggi,' she added quickly as Maggi stiffened de-
fensively. 'When he entered our lives three years ago,

he was in a very bad way. He had lost you, and your child, and it was probably seeing his complete desolation at the fact that brought me to my senses where my own marriage was concerned.

'A child of my own had been my obsession for over two years, so much so that I had forgotten it was Geoffrey I loved, that it was our relationship, our marriage, that was important. Seeing Adam, how he grieved for what he had lost, at least brought me to my senses concerning that. It was also because of him that Geoffrey and I went ahead with the idea of adoption. Adam made me realise how lucky I was to have Geoffrey, the other half of myself, and that I would love any child the two of us brought up together,' she added emotionally.

Maggi swallowed hard. 'I never knew Adam was like that.'

'Because you wouldn't listen to him,' Celia chided gently. 'I can't blame you for that; sometimes the person closest to you isn't the one you listen to but the one on whom you take out your pain and hurt. That's what I did with Geoffrey.'

And what Maggi had done with Adam? Had she done that, after the accident, after the loss of the baby, when she'd been told there might not be any more children? If so, perhaps Adam couldn't be blamed for turning to someone else, someone who would show him a little warmth and understanding!

'You've seen Daniel, Maggi,' Celia continued. 'Believe me, Michael is just as beautiful, because they're identical twins. I've loved the two of them since they came to us at six weeks old. They're ours, Maggi, mine and Geoffrey's, because we have loved them, nursed them when they weren't well, laughed with them when they did something funny. Being a parent isn't just about biologically carrying a child; true love begins once they're born and become real people to you. I couldn't love Daniel and Michael any more than I do now,' she added simply. 'They're our children, Maggi, and they always have been.'

Maggi understood what she was saying, accepted it, but her marriage to Adam hadn't been the same. 'Adam left me, Celia,' she said abruptly. 'Not the other way round.'

'Have you ever asked him why?' the other woman persisted. 'Because I certainly did. The man loved you, so why would he leave you—even if you had told him to?'

'And?' She held her breath as she waited for the answer.

'Oh, no, Maggi.' Celia shook her head regretfully. 'Adam is my friend. I won't break his confidences to me. If you want to know the answer to that, you'll have to ask him yourself.'

'He isn't here to ask,' Maggi pointed out bluntly.

Celia gave her a sympathetic look. 'Then you'll have to go to his home yourself and ask him. Would that really be so difficult to do, Maggi?' She paused as Maggi visibly paled, then went on, 'Hasn't Adam been the one, up to now, to do all the running after you? It almost killed him waiting for the day he knew you would be singing again, so that he could finally come back into your life.'

'He was horrible at the music festival,' Maggi re-called. 'Every inch his arrogant self.'

Celia gave her a pitying look. 'How long were you married to him, Maggi? Two years, I believe.' She answered her own question. 'And you never got to know him at all—'

'Yes, I did, damn you!' Maggi defended heatedly. 'And he was loving, and fun to be with—until something didn't go his way!'

'And how often did that happen?' the other woman prompted softly.

Not very often. They had been so much in tune with each other, emotionally, physically, professionally, that nothing had really gone wrong in their marriage until the accident—and then everything had gone wrong! But had that been because of Adam or because of her? Had Adam changed—or had she?

'Maggi, I'm going to give you Adam's address—if you don't already have it—'

'I don't,' she said quickly.

Celia nodded, standing up. 'Very few people do. He's been like an angry lion living there, licking his wounds.' She wrote on the pad lying next to the telephone. 'It's up to you whether or not you go and see him.' She handed Maggi a slip of paper. 'But I'm almost positive he won't come to you. Not again. Isn't it worth just one more conversation together before you finally call it a day?'

'The divorce is almost complete,' Maggi told her distractedly.

'Divorces can be undone,' Celia dismissed easily. 'What do you have to lose, Maggi?'

Nothing. Not any more. She loved Adam, knew she would never love anyone else as much as she loved him. But could she actually go to his home, risk being rejected on the doorstep? Could she try to speak to him, to forge some sort of friendship between them? Wouldn't that be better than nothing at all?

'You're a nice woman, Celia.' Maggi hugged her. 'And a good friend to Adam.'

'You believe that's all I am now?' She laughed as Maggi looked uncomfortable. 'Reporters have never heard of a man and woman being just friends; Geoffrey and I have both been well aware of the rumours going around about Adam and myself—in fact we've all had a good laugh about it. I'm a one-man woman, Maggi, and Geoffrey is that man.'

'I'm sorry—'

'Don't be,' Celia dismissed. 'Having Adam reputed to be my lover has done wonders for my image!' She touched Maggi's cheek lightly. 'But I'm your friend too, Maggi; always remember that. No matter what happens.'

Maggi wasn't sure she deserved the other woman's generosity after the uncharitable thoughts she had harboured against her.

Did she deserve to have Adam listen to her either? she wondered as she sat in a taxi on the way to his home. What did she have to say to him that he would want to listen to?

That night, after they had made love, she had wondered if Adam loved her. Did he? Or was that hoping for too much? Even if, by some miracle, he did still love her, could they work out their differences and go on from there?

Yes, of course they could! Love *had* to be the deciding factor in all this. It could forgive, if not forget, anything...

CHAPTER TWELVE

MAGGI didn't feel quite so confident as she stood on the other side of Adam's door, waiting for him to answer the ring of the bell! Perhaps he hadn't come straight home. Perhaps he had—

'Magdalena!' Adam opened the door and looked stunned to see her standing there, obviously the last person he expected to see.

Which wasn't surprising; she hadn't exactly given the impression earlier that she ever wanted to see him again, and now she was here, at his home, of her own volition.

Where he lived was something of a surprise to her. She had expected he would live in a luxurious apartment somewhere, but instead he owned a three-floor Victorian house in an elegant area of London. Alone, if the fact that he had answered the door himself was anything to go by. And by alone she meant there appeared to be no housekeeper, or anyone else, in fact, who would care for him and the house. Which probably meant he had chosen to do that for himself...

Maggi didn't know what to say to him now that the time had actually come!

He raised his eyebrows at her silence. 'Do you want to come in, or have you changed your mind?' he ventured.

'I—' She cleared her throat as her voice came out

as a choked squeak. 'I'll come in—if that's all right with you?'

'Be my guest.' He stood back with exaggerated politeness to usher her in. 'Come through.' He passed her to enter a room to the left of the hallway.

Maggi went into what was obviously his 'den', where there were bookcases filled untidily with books, dozens of cassettes littering the table, and several comfortable chairs also littered with newspapers and books.

Adam moved without haste to clear one of those chairs for her to sit down. 'I haven't got any tidier, I'm afraid,' he told her dryly.

It used to be a joke between them that one day she would find him buried under his own debris.

She sat down heavily. 'This is a lovely house,' she said. What was she doing here? Was she about to make the biggest fool of herself?

'What are you doing here?' Adam ignored her politeness, seeming instead to read her panicked thoughts.

She swallowed hard. 'I—I'm not really sure,' she admitted ruefully.

Adam stood looking down at her. 'Did you talk to Celia?' he asked hardly.

She looked up at him with unwavering blue eyes. 'Not in the way I think you mean, no.'

'Your father, then,' he pressed. 'Have you spoken to him?'

Maggi shook her head, frowning. 'I came straight here from Celia's,' she told him slowly. 'She's nice, by the way, obviously a good friend to you. I meant that exactly the way I said it, Adam,' she added firmly as his mouth tightened. 'But I'm curious about my father; what could he possibly want to talk to me about concerning you?'

Adam turned away. 'I've told you before. It isn't important—'

'It is to me,' she said with feeling, standing up again, at too much of a disadvantage being seated while he stood. 'Adam, it wasn't easy for me to come here, and now that I am—Adam, we need to talk. Really talk, instead of just arguing all the time.'

'And whose fault is that?' he challenged.

She sighed. 'At the moment, yours!' she told him pointedly.

He glared. 'Does Mark know you're here?'

Mark…? Of course—Adam still thought she was romantically involved with his cousin. 'You really should keep up with the family news, Adam,' she said evenly. 'In three weeks' time, unlike you, I will be singing and dancing at Mark's wedding.'

'God, the two of you aren't wasting any time are you?' Adam burst out disgustedly. 'After telling me you wouldn't marry him, you're now going through with it before the ink is even dry on our divorce papers! You—'

'As his bridesmaid.' Maggi finished what she had been saying, her gaze easily holding Adam's. 'Mark has been engaged to my physiotherapist for the last year, Adam,' she explained. 'He and Andrea are getting married soon.'

'But he said— You said—'

'*You* said, Adam,' Maggi corrected him firmly. 'I

never actually said I was involved with Mark; you
have just always assumed I was.'

'You never denied it,' Adam accused her. 'Neither
of you did,' he added angrily.

'You were always so willing to believe the worst,
and—well, in truth, it was easier on my part to let
you go on thinking that.'

His eyes narrowed. 'Why?'

They were facing each other across the room like
adversaries, and it wasn't how Maggi wanted things
to be. There had been too much antagonism already,
and it had brought them to this angry point.

'Adam.' She swallowed hard, willing herself to
carry on. 'How did you feel when I lost the baby three
years ago?'

He stiffened. 'That's history, Magdalena,' he said
grimly.

His continued use of her full name gave her encouragement. 'It's our history, Adam, and I need to
know. It's when our problems began, and—I need to
know,' she repeated huskily.

He gave a heavy sigh. 'The loss of our baby was—
devastating.'

She felt her heart sink. It was as she had thought,
then; losing the baby had changed things between
them for ever.

'But not as devastating as losing you would have
been,' Adam went on. 'It was sad to lose the baby,
and I know how deeply it affected you, but—a child
can never be as real to a man during pregnancy as it
is to a woman. Once it's born, it's a different matter,
but during pregnancy we have none of the advantages

of feeling that life growing inside us. We can't really bond with the baby the way a mother does until it's actually born and we can hold it in our arms.

'It was our child, Magdalena, and I loved it. And to lose him in the way we did—!' He bowed his head. 'But if it had been you that had died, then I would have lost everything.' His mouth twisted with bitterness. 'As it turned out, I did that anyway!'

'Why?' She held her breath, almost couldn't breathe for the tightness constricting her chest.

He sighed wearily. 'You tell me. You were the one who couldn't stand to have me around, the one whose health and mental welfare deteriorated every time I visited—to such a degree that in the end the hospital thought it better if I stayed away. The distress my presence caused you was seriously hindering your recovery,' he remembered.

'Is that—?' She swallowed hard again, her mouth suddenly dry. 'Is that why you turned to Sue Castle? I'm not blaming you for that, Adam,' she added quickly as his face darkened ominously. 'I just need to know.'

'I never "turned to" Sue Castle,' he told her firmly. 'We sang together for a while. But that's all. I never understood how you came to that conclusion.'

'I spoke to her.' Maggi moistened her lips. 'She told me—she said—'

'She said what?' Adam prompted harshly. 'When did she speak to you?' he added, more slowly.

'The morning after— When you didn't come home that night because of the snow. I…' Her lips felt stiff and unmoving, making it difficult for her to talk at all. She drew in a deeply controlling breath. 'I tele-phoned the hotel you said you were staying at. They put me through to your bedroom and— Sue an-swered.' There were tears in her eyes as she looked at him.

'Sue did?' He looked puzzled. 'But—'

'She said she was sorry, but that these things hap-pened sometimes when you worked closely with someone.' Maggi swallowed down her tears. 'I—I felt as if my world had finally come to an end,' she ad-mitted haltingly.

Adam was still puzzled. 'We're talking about the night we were caught in London by a snowstorm? Is that the night?'

'You know it is,' Maggi choked. 'It was the only night you were actually gone all night, and I—I called the next morning to say hello, to see whether or not you would be able to make it home that day. I never actually spoke to you—because after what Sue had said I—I couldn't!' She shook her head. 'I felt so betrayed that night, Adam, so let down. But I'm older now, and not as emotionally vulnerable as I was then. I realise that these things do happen, that some-times—'

'Not to me,' Adam cut in. 'Not then. And not now. I want to know—'

'What do you mean, ''not now''?' She gave him a startled look. Surely Adam had been involved with someone during the last three years? Hadn't he…?

'That isn't important just now,' he dismissed im-patiently.

'It is to me,' she protested. Surely Adam couldn't

have been as celibate as she had for the last three years? It was incredible if he had...

He nodded. 'We'll discuss it in a moment. Right now it's more important that we talk about Sue Castle. What the hell was she doing in my hotel room that morning? I don't— Wait a minute,' he said slowly, some of the thunderous darkness leaving his brow. 'I met her downstairs in the restaurant for breakfast, and while I was at the desk she went upstairs to collect our guitars from our rooms. *Rooms*, Magdalena. What time did you telephone?'

'I don't remember exactly.' She stopped and thought for a moment. 'But it was early. I hadn't been able to sleep all night, and—I remember now. It was about seven-thirty,' she recalled. 'I waited until then so that I wouldn't disturb your sleep. You had been working so hard, and rushing back to my parents' house in between, and I—I wanted to leave you to sleep as long as I could.' The shock she had felt when Sue had answered the telephone had never left her.

'You wouldn't have disturbed me, Magdalena, because I couldn't sleep anyway!' Adam told her ruefully. 'I was awake all night worrying about you, whether or not you were okay. It was like a slap in the face when I got to your parents' house and you told me you had spent all night thinking about our marriage and had decided it was over, that we had nothing left to give each other.' He looked sad.

She *had* said those things, but only because— 'Did you ever have an affair with Sue Castle?'

Adam's gaze locked unwaveringly with hers. 'No.'

'Oh, God...!' She sank down into the chair, her legs suddenly feeling weak.

Adam watched her, frowning darkly. 'Do you believe me?'

She looked up at him, her gaze as unwavering as his had been seconds ago. 'Yes.'

He let out a shaky sigh, coming down on his haunches beside her chair. 'Is that the only reason you told me those things three years ago?' he prompted huskily. 'Is that why you told me to go?'

The tears were threatening to fall once again. 'Not—completely. It was everything,' she choked as he looked at her questioningly. 'I couldn't walk, couldn't have more children, wasn't the person you had married...'

'Our marriage vows said "in sickness and in health", Magdalena.' Adam took both her hands into the warm strength of his own. 'I meant that when I said it. And I still mean it,' he added softly. 'I've kept our marriage vows, Magdalena. All of them,' he added meaningfully.

There *hadn't* been anyone else in his life in the last three years!

Maggi looked at him searchingly, couldn't miss the complete commitment in his face. 'But you never came back,' she said in a small voice. 'Not to see me. Or to see if I had changed my mind—'

'Your father assured me that you hadn't. Yes, I've kept in touch with Ted on and off for the last three years.' He answered her unasked question. 'He assured me you were still adamant you had made a mistake in marrying me, that you refused to even have my name mentioned in the house.'

She had, but she hadn't known—

'I had no idea you spoke to my father,' she said agitatedly. Her father had never mentioned it—never. Could this be the reason why her father had desperately wanted to talk to both of them when he was in hospital? Could it have been the strain of the secret he had kept from her that had caused his heart attack in the first place? Thinking back, she realised her father had begun to look ill from the time he'd known she had seen Adam at the music festival...

'I wanted to know how you were, Magdalena,' Adam told her gruffly.

'And my refusal to talk about you was a self-defence mechanism,' she burst out emotionally. 'It hurt too much!'

'It hurt me too, to know that your recovery was all the quicker without my presence,' Adam remembered. 'But I had to know you were getting better. I needed to know!'

'Why?' She held her breath, almost afraid of the answer but at the same time longing for it.

'I hoped that once you were better—once you were well again...I intended seeing you—whether you wanted to see me again or not!' His expression softened. 'I know you think I'm arrogant and proud— Yes, you do,' he murmured as she would have protested. 'But where you're concerned I've never had any pride. I love you, Magdalena. I've always loved you. I always will.'

'Oh, Adam...!' She buried her face in her hands,

the tears falling unchecked now at the thought of what he must have gone through over the last three years. She had suffered herself, but nothing like this...! 'I've made such a mess of things,' she sobbed. 'I thought you didn't love me as I was, that you had found someone else, and I couldn't bear the thought of that. For a while I think I even hated you,' she admitted brokenly.

'I'm sure you convinced your father that was exactly the way you felt,' Adam acknowledged carefully. 'He's been so protective of you. But I know he felt sorry for me too, which was why he bothered with me at all. But he wasn't about to let me near you. Although when he came to see me that day he seemed to think something had changed...' He frowned. 'Unfortunately, he collapsed before we could really talk properly.'

Maggi swallowed hard—swallowed her own pride. It had brought her nothing but unhappiness these last three years! Because it was pride that had made her close her heart to this man, shut her eyes to the truth. *She* was the one who hadn't been able to bear her inability to walk; it had been easier to reject Adam, exclude him from her life, than to face life with him with herself as a cripple.

'My father had probably guessed...' She cleared her throat, her voice thick with emotion. 'He had probably realised that I had been lying all those years, that I still loved you. Because I do, Adam,' she told him in a rush. 'I love you very much. I always have. And I always will.' She unabashedly echoed his own words.

Adam had looked pained as she spoke, but now relief and love flooded unrestrained into his face. 'Enough to marry me?' he prompted.

She gave a tearful smile. 'We're still married.' Their decree absolute wouldn't come through for several more weeks yet.

'Will you marry me again, Magdalena?' he persisted firmly. '"Love, honour—"'

'"And obey"?' she cut in teasingly, still only half believing she was being given this second chance at happiness.

'"And obey"!' he echoed as he pulled her easily to her feet. 'That way there won't be a repeat of the last three years; I'll just tell you to stay put in future, until we've sorted out whatever problem we might have! Not that I think we'll have that many; I've always been easy to live with,' he added wryly.

Maggi gave a shaky laugh as she moved into his arms. 'Perfect,' she agreed.

Adam gave a triumphant laugh before sweeping her close against him. 'Only someone who really loved me could possibly say that!' he murmured, before his mouth claimed hers.

They shared the intensity of their love in that kiss, all the pent-up emotion of the last three years finally being allowed to fly free. It engulfed them both in flames so intense, they threatened to consume the pair of them.

'I'm not letting you leave me again, Magdalena,' Adam told her as she sat on his knee in the armchair. 'Not even for a minute. You'll stay here with me tonight, and tomorrow we'll start making the arrange-

ments to reaffirm our wedding vows. A new beginning, Magdalena.'

'I'm not arguing,' she pointed out gently, her head
resting on his shoulder.

'That makes a change,' he muttered.

She laughed softly. 'Doesn't it?' She settled more
comfortably into his arms. 'This feels so good, Adam.
We've been so at odds with each other for so long…!'
She snuggled into his neck, just enjoying the warmth
and smell of him.

'I think you should go ahead with the launch of
your solo album, Magdalena,' he told her gently. 'I
think you've earnt it.'

'And afterwards?'

'That's up to you.' He shrugged. 'I'm not pushing
for anything any more. I have you back in my life;
that's enough.'

'I want to sing with you again, Adam. I want that
very much,' she said with feeling.

His arms tightened. 'We've really only ever needed
each other, haven't we, Magdalena?'

She raised her head to look at him. 'Does that mean
you don't want us to have children?'

His expression darkened. 'Despite how well adoption has turned out for Celia and Geoffrey, I don't
intend to push that option either. If it isn't what you
want.'

'How about a child of our own?' Once again she
found she was holding her breath as she waited for
his answer.

His expression softened. 'You know that isn't possible.'

'The doctors didn't think it would be possible after the accident,' she acknowledged. 'The internal damage was quite extensive. But—they've monitored me really closely since that time, carried out tests, and—well, there's a chance, they said—a remote chance. Don't look like that, Adam,' she said quickly as he began to frown again. 'Celia told me how obsessive she became concerning having her own child. I'm not about to become like that. In fact, I—I could be pregnant already,' she added shyly. 'I—it's been five weeks since we—and I haven't—'

'Magdalena, I'm your husband; I'm not unconversant with the monthly cycle of your body. I'm not unconversant with your body at all,' he added teasingly. 'Are you saying you haven't had a period since the night we made love?'

'Yes!' She sat up, smiling at him glowingly. 'I didn't even realise until earlier this evening, when it suddenly occurred to me that maybe—just possibly—I might be pregnant, Adam!' she said tremulously. 'I just might!'

'And if you are I'll be ecstatic, Magdalena,' he told her huskily. 'But even if you aren't I'm ecstatic anyway. All I've ever needed is you, to love you and to have you love me in return.'

'I do. So much, Adam. So very much,' she told him sincerely as their lips and bodies melded together in perfect harmony.

And their love for each other overflowed the day their daughter was born, eight months later.

MILLS & BOON®

Next Month's Romances

Each month you can choose from a wide variety of romance novels from Mills & Boon. Below are the new titles to look out for next month from the Presents™ and Enchanted™ series.

Presents™

A NANNY FOR CHRISTMAS	Sara Craven
A FORBIDDEN DESIRE	Robyn Donald
THE WINTER BRIDE	Lynne Graham
THE PERFECT MATCH?	Penny Jordan
RED-HOT AND RECKLESS	Miranda Lee
BARGAIN WITH THE WIND	Kathleen O'Brien
THE DISOBEDIENT BRIDE	Elizabeth Power
ALL MALE	Kay Thorpe

Enchanted™

SANTA'S SPECIAL DELIVERY	Val Daniels
THE MARRIAGE PACT	Elizabeth Duke
A MIRACLE FOR CHRISTMAS	Grace Green
ACCIDENTAL WIFE	Day Leclaire
ONE NIGHT BEFORE CHRISTMAS	Catherine Leigh
A SINGULAR HONEYMOON	Leigh Michaels
A HUSBAND FOR CHRISTMAS	Emma Richmond
TEMPORARY GIRLFRIEND	Jessica Steele

RISING
Tides

EMILIE RICHARDS

**The reading of a woman's will threatens to
destroy her family**

As a hurricane gathers strength, the reading of
Aurore Gerritsen's will threatens to expose dark
secrets and destroy her family. Emilie Richards
continues the saga of a troubled family with
Rising Tides, the explosive sequel to the critically
acclaimed *Iron Lace*.

**AVAILABLE IN PAPERBACK
FROM OCTOBER 1997**

FREE!

FOUR FREE
specially selected
Presents™ novels
PLUS a FREE Mystery Gift
when you return this page...

Return this coupon and we'll send you 4 Mills & Boon® romances from the Presents series and a mystery gift absolutely FREE! We'll even pay the postage and packing for you.

We're making you this offer to introduce you to the benefits of the Reader Service™– FREE home delivery of brand-new Mills & Boon Presents novels, at least a month before they are available in the shops, FREE gifts and a monthly Newsletter packed with information, competitions, author profiles and lots more...

Accepting these FREE books and gift places you under no obligation to buy, you may cancel at any time, even after receiving just your free shipment. Simply complete the coupon below and send it to:

MILLS & BOON READER SERVICE, FREEPOST, CROYDON, SURREY, CR9 3WZ.

READERS IN EIRE PLEASE SEND COUPON TO PO BOX 4546, DUBLIN 24

NO STAMP NEEDED

Yes, please send me 4 free Presents novels and a mystery gift. I understand that unless you hear from me, I will receive 6 superb new titles every month for just £2.20* each, postage and packing free. I am under no obligation to purchase any books and I may cancel or suspend my subscription at any time, but the free books and gift will be mine to keep in any case. (I am over 18 years of age)

P7YE

Ms/Mrs/Miss/Mr_____
BLOCK CAPS PLEASE

Address_____

_____

_____ Postcode _____

Jennifer
BLAKE

GARDEN
of
SCANDAL

She wants her life back...

Branded a murderer, Laurel Bancroft has
been a recluse for years. Now she wants her
life back—but someone in her past will do
anything to ensure the truth stays buried.

*"Blake's style is as steamy as a still July
night...as overwhelmingly hot as Cajun spice."*
—Chicago Tribune

**AVAILABLE IN PAPERBACK
FROM NOVEMBER 1997**

GET TO KNOW

THE BEST OF ENEMIES

the latest blockbuster from TAYLOR SMITH

Who would you trust with your life? Think again.

*Linked to a terrorist bombing, a young student goes
missing. One woman believes in the girl's innocence
and is determined to find her before she is silenced.
Leya Nash has to decide—quickly—who to trust.
The wrong choice could be fatal.*

50ᵖ OFF
COUPON
VALID UNTIL: 28.2.1998

TAYLOR SMITH'S *THE BEST OF ENEMIES*

9 904170 200509 >

0472 00189